Philip Abraham

Autumn Gatherings

Philip Abraham

Autumn Gatherings

ISBN/EAN: 9783337367305

Printed in Europe, USA, Canada, Australia, Japan

Cover: Foto ©Andreas Hilbeck / pixelio.de

More available books at **www.hansebooks.com**

AUTUMN GATHERINGS,

BEING

A Collection of Prose and Poetry.

SACRED AND SECULAR.

BY

PHILIP ABRAHAM.

"When Autumn scatters his departing gleams,
Warn'd of approaching Winter."
Thomson.

PUBLISHED BY AND FOR THE AUTHOR, AT

147, GOWER STREET, LONDON, W.C.

—

1866.

CONTENTS.

CONTENTS.

AUTUMN GATHERINGS.

———◆———

THE SOUL.

A Paraphrase of אלהי נשמה שנתת בי

Morning Service.

My God! the soul Thou hast given me,
Is robed in vestal purity;
Pure from Thee it emanated,
So was it by Thy will created—
As richest boon from Heaven bequeathed,
By Thee 'twas formed—in me was breathed;
By Thee inspired; while life remains,
In me Thy might that soul sustains:
In time, the gift from Thee which came,
Wilt Thou at Thine own hour reclaim;
Again to be restored to me,
Immortal in Eternity.

Be then my care, each transient hour,
To praise Thy name, to own Thy power;
My Fathers' God! Almighty Thou!
Before Thy will all creatures bow;

B

Omnipotent ! all dost Thou control,
Dread Sovereign Thou, of life and soul ;
That soul, Thy mercy erst did send,
That Heaven with earthly mould might blend ;
That life we render, till Thy breath,
Proclaims a life that knows no death ;
Revives the lifeless corpse once more,
And does to man his soul restore :
O blessed be Thy name e'ermore !

——o——

PSALM XXIX.

EXORDIUM.

Ye on earth who mighty are,
  Give each day, each praiseful hour,
Give to Him, more mighty far,
  Honour, glory, strength and power.

Give unto His holy Name,
  Homage due with voice and lyre ;
Loud the hallowed God proclaim,
  Worship Him in rich attire.

———

Voices o'er the waters break,
  Dread His thunders thrill the deep ;
Floods 'neath Glory's God now quake,
  Awed they from His presence leap.

Forth the Voice of God rebounds,
  Charged with all subduing might ;
Majesty pervades its sounds,
  Quivering forests shrink in fright.

Cedars feel the voice, and quail,
  Proud which stood in Lebanon;
See, God's voice the trees assail,
  Shivered cedars' pride is gone.

Skipping like some youthful steer,
  Joying in its strength new-born,
Doth Lebanon itself uprear,
  Eke Sirion as the unicorn.

Piercing thro' the fire-fed flame,
  Cleaving way God's voice doth make,
Kadesh shrinks as tho' in shame,
  Howling wastes that voice doth shake.

Hinds then calve in pain and throe,
  Forests stand no more concealed,
Speaks the voice, and answering, lo!
  Shines His glory forth revealed.

Filled with praise the sacred fanes,
  There they chant the votive prayer;
God! He sway o'er floods maintains,
  King! He reigns for e'er and e'er.

Strength He to His nation gives,
  Blessèd, bids their ranks increase;
Pleased the tidings each receives,
  "His people He will bless with peace."

CONSOLATION.

אאמצכם במו פי וניד שפתי יחשך

"I would strengthen you with my mouth, and the moving of my
lips should assuage your grief." (Job xvi. 5).

FRET not nor repine, when pain or lengthened woe,
Sinks the lone heart with sad oppression's blow;
Discipline thy soul with calm to bear resigned,
The common lot of grief, foredoomed mankind.
Why hope to shun the heritage of life,
Thy share of anxious toil or raging strife?
Why seek to 'scape the universal doom,
That spreads a shade o'er man of darkened gloom?
With life comes woe, in birth is death's first germ,*
And lengthened years but misery's lengthened term.
What hope secure can mortal joys afford,
Pendant o'er all, there hangs a glittering sword;
A film sustains, it quivers at a breath;
Now gorgeous pomp, and now relentless death.

Look round the world, can'st single one of all,
Who shares not in the curse of Adam's fall?
Lives there the man, who free from pain or ill,
Maintains unchecked the purpose of his will?
Fearless in power, triumphant conquerors ride,
A nation's shoutings sound their names in pride;

* — Man, perhaps the moment of his breath,
Receives the lurking principles of death.   POPE.

Can laurel wreaths avert the aching head?
In purple robes do palsied limbs ne'er tread?
The roseate colours tint the hero's cheek;
Does blanching grief within his heart ne'er speak?
Oh, who can say, where rolls that ivory car,
And incense burns, and flowers are scatter'd far,
What thorns may pierce, what thoughts their pangs
    inflict?
What Ghosts of buried years his soul afflict?

Wanton and warm, voluptuous beauties clasp;
Glory and empire seek to court his grasp:
How long can beauty charm whom age assails?
His trembling hand to wield the sceptre fails.
To do him homage crouching suppliants wait,
Can they one pang assuage—retard his fate?
Where viands rare to tempt the taste compete,
Does no "one drop" embitter every sweet?
Where softest couch in banquet halls is pressed,
Sits no "black care" an uninvited guest?

Fret not nor repine. The sage who woos the night,
Whom science guides with all-illuming light,
Whom no ambition tempts, no passions lure,
Whose joy in Wisdom's page might seem secure,
When dearly earn'd some knowledge anxious sought,
Hath mourned to find his boasted knowledge nought.
The wisest sage, whom God himself endowed,
Hath Wisdom's grief in bitter pangs avowed.*
Imperfect nature, more it seeks to know,
The more it loads its weight of cumbrous woe;
Most sad is he, who aims to raise his kind,
With ardent love for man's best aid designed;

* Ecclesiastes, i. 18, etc.

Wasting in cheerless hope his vigorous hours,
Who shall recruit his now exhausted powers?
A sad eclipse obscured his brightest dawn,
Cold hearts have spurned because he could not fawn;
"His days are sorrows, all his labours grief," *
And best from struggling life were death relief.

Who joys, must grieve—who lives, must see decay;
Affections—kindred-ties—must pass away:
The tax we pay to live, as years roll on,
Is everlasting sorrow.   One by one,
The little child—the playmate of our youth—
Our dearest friendships—she of changeless truth—
Our honoured sires—our venerated guides—
Pass from our vision—vanish from our sides;
And, like the fabled mother, turned to stone,
We stand bereaved—in misery—alone!

FRET not nor repine.   Though man be doomed to ill,
Who shall control the purpose of His will?
Who dare impugn Omnipotent design?
Through all be sure there reigns a good Divine.
The purest silver, shining radiant white,
From furnace heat first won its splendour bright;
What mingled dross, what worthless ore commixed,
In yon rude mass by Nature's hand seemed fixed;
Purged in the fire, where round the fierce heat glowed,
Freed from alloy,† refined, the metal flowed.
God loves the world; when most His chastening hand
Would seem to smite, could man then understand,
How not to wound, but save, that blow is meant,
And but to purge from sin, is sorrow sent.

* Ecclesiastes, ii. 23.   † Isaiah i. 25.

Adversity but tries us, through its furnace-fire,
Sublimed from earth to heaven we aspire.
Lowly then kneel, and humbly kiss the rod;
Can ill, FOR ILL ALONE, emerge from God?
A purpose reigns, and all for mankind's good;
If man were prescient, this were understood;
For Saints when erring, them He first reproves,
And those whom most He chastens, most He loves.

———o———

THE KISS OF PURITY.

"And when the unconscious infant smiled,
I kissed it for its mother's sake."　　　BYRON.

I KISSED that fair and favoured child,
　But not for the infant's sake;
Though well its look, so pure and mild,
　Might fond affection wake.

I looked not at its gentle face,
　Pure Innocence' own dwelling;
Scarce gazed I at each budding grace,
　All beauteous charms foretelling.

It raised to me its little arms,
　And pouting outstretched lips;
And there were treasured honied charms,
　Sweet as the queen-bee sips.

For there was hived a fond embrace,
  A mother's thoughts revealing,
As bending o'er its lovely face,
  Affection's kiss was sealing.

And chance, thought I, as radiance bright,
  Gleams in the twilight darkling,
Perhaps some ray of Virtue's light
  Might still for me be sparkling.

Then too, I thought, as evil fled,
  When touched by Edward's* finger,
That on those lips so roseate-red,
  Some purity might linger;

Might charm away each lurking ill,
  More chastened thoughts fresh bringing,
As plants, once withered, near the rill,
  Again in odour springing.

——o——

THE SCEPTIC AND THE SAGE.

(AN EPIGRAM.)

" If there no Future be," the Sceptic cries,
  " How vain your boasted hope, your self-denying."
" If there a Future is," the Sage replies,
  " How dread the cheating thought *your* hope
    supplying."

* The Confessor.

"SOMETHING AFTER DEATH."

(IMITATED FROM A TRANSLATION OF PLATO.)

I WERE to blame, if seeing death approach,
I felt no fearful dread, no chilling awe ;
But that I firmly think a better state
Awaits the men who goodly die, and go
At first to other gods, both wise and good ;
And then to nobler men themselves precede.
Therefore, with earnest hope those dead to meet,
I welcome death, and feel in heart assured,
There still remains a life for them who die ;
And better for the good than those who sin.

———o———

PSALM CXXXVII.

By Babel's streams, when seated there,
   Our hearts with our loved Zion fraught,
Weeping in grief, o'erwhelmed with care,
   Still Zion filled our every thought.

Our harps, now all their music stilled,
   Hung silent on the willows round ;
Our voices, though melodious skilled,
   Could now no more in joy resound.

When there our captors us did ask,
   And bade us mirth and gladness bring ;
Yea, there our spoilers did us task,
   That we of Zion's songs should sing.

Oh, how can we in stranger land,
   The song of our loved God uptake?
Oh, how can we, a captive band,
   The holy hymn of joy awake?

Jerusalem; if e'er forgot,
   Thy blest, thy lov'd, thy honoured soil,
If Salem's thoughts I treasure not,
   Then be my right hand's strength a spoil.

When Memory fails to think of thee,
   My tongue shall to my palate cleave;
All joys above shall Salem be,
   'Mid every joy for thee I grieve.

O God! remember and requite,
   Whom in Jerusalem's saddened days,
When Edom's sons did shout in spite,
   To earth did our foundations raze.

Proud Babel's daughter now elate,
   How bless'd, renowned, that man will be,
Who hurls thee from thy pomp and state,
   And doth our cause avenge on thee.

All hail to him, whose ruthless grasp,
   Where round thy smiling infants flock,
Their hands shall from thy neck unclasp,
   And dash them quivering 'gainst the rock.

———o———

WHO IS TOO YOUNG?

אל תאמר נער אנכי כי על כל אשר אשלחך תלך

"Say not, I am a youth; for thou shalt go to all that I shall send
thee." (Jerem. i. 7.)

Say not, "I am a youth, therefore unskill'd,
God's will to do, His holy law to keep";
In early youth who sows, in age shall reap,
And see with precious grain his store-house filled.
Would'st glean luxuriant crop in hour of need?
Think not to idly waste thy spring-tide now,
Nor fallow leave the soil that needs the plough,
The harden'd clods to break or free from weed.
Within thy mind implant the will to do,
What though at best the tender graft be weak,
Trailing its tendrils firm support will seek,
And gathering strength its vigorous growth pursue :
Reason developed aids the tender shoot ;
Perception conscious bends its course to light,
And Wisdom's sap the stem endows with might,
In clustering stores to yield its priceless fruit.

"Say not I am a child and cannot speak ;"
Whereto the Lord thy missive steps shall send,
There go resolved, thereto thy purpose bend,
Nor fear to fail tho' humble thou and weak.
Strengthen thy faith nor doubt sufficient help,
Thine armour gird, thy panoply of truth :
Who saved from giant's power the Hebrew youth,
From out the paw of bear or lion's whelp,

E'en He thy helper is; but will to do.
That shepherd boy had early taught his tongue,
The votive lays which Zion's monarch sung,
And bade in gladsome age his "youth renew."
Fill full thy heart with generous impulse free,
Excite, encourage every nobler aim;
Who knows how soon thy duty's call may claim,
Or, what the after-man, lives, child in thee.
The little Samuel heard revealed a voice;
" Eli perceived the Lord had called the child,"
Foresaw the prophet in the infant mild,
And bade the chosen seer of God rejoice.
Rest in God's temple, when His voice may call,
Minist'ring there in snow white garments clad,
Thy heart shall hear with holy rapture glad;
And so no ill shall e'er thy steps befall.

Yes! nerve thy soul betimes.   Well, early taught,
Was he, indulgent-nursed and favoured boy,
Who torn from home and reft of every joy,
To manhood's cares ere manhood's years was brought.
Was he "too young" in virtue's track to steer?
Temptation's wiles had lured him to his harm,
But deaf to syren voice or baneful charm,
" He feared his God and knew no other fear;" *
Nor dungeon's depths, nor regal palace hall,
" Disturbed the even tenor of his mind,"
As captive slave or monarch's friend resigned,
The Hebrew youth saw Heaven's hand in all.

* " Je crains Dieu, cher Abner, et n'ai point d'autre crainte."
RACINE.

Yea! e'en "from mouth of babes and sucklings' lips,*
Is strength ordained" and God-like wisdom taught.
How oft with words with sweet allurement fraught,
(Pure eloquence, which practised art outstrips,)
The young has led the aged; the weak, the strong;
Children when honored are their parents' pride,
Who walk unharm'd where foes malign deride; †
The virtuous child preserves his sire from wrong.
The puny rill will widen to the brook,
The brook expands and fills a river's shores;
Onward, unchecked the rapid stream now pours;
This mighty power from yon sequestered nook.
If chance had stemmed the streamlet at its course,
Where now had been the river's useful tide?
Who had its banks with liquid wealth supplied,
If, failing strength, it faltered in its force?
Thy life, my son, so like that sheltered rill,
Glides yet unheeded—but await the hour,
Matured in years, invigorate in power;
Thou shalt thy purposed course in all fulfil.
Let so thy deeds—the utterance of thy tongue,
Flow gently smooth and shape their onward way,
Well pleased, when called, thy Maker's will obey,
Nor fear thy strength too weak, thy years too young.

——o——

TO A NEW-BORN INFANT.

When first through life's new paths you stray,
   And pause to gaze on all you view,
So guide through life your glorious way,
   That all may pause to gaze on you.

* Psalm viii.   † Psalm cxxvii.

LOVE.

Who bids the earth to move; the spangled sky
Who bids to shine; their vernal green afresh
The trees who bids renew; with instinct rare,
Joy-seeking birds their raptur'd mates to choose?
E'en He who bids us love. Of earthly growth
It never came; 't was kindly Heaven sent,
Of Heaven's gifts the first—the woes of man
To soothe with dulcet balm. Were Love away,
Then Life were but a doom of endless death;
But bless'd with Love, we deem each hour an age.

—o—

THE RIVERS OF HELL.

(TO A LADY.)

E'en Phlegethon, when shared with thee,
Would seem Elysian groves to me;
And Acheron, though black as night,
With thee would beam Olympus bright.
In vain I seek the power of Styx,
Invulnerate my heart to fix;
For Lethe's waters bring to me,
Forgetfulness of all—but thee.

TO A LADY.

(THE WRITER DECLINING A RELIGIOUS DISCUSSION.)

Say! why should'st thou think but a moment I cherish,
    One thought that could breathe against Purity's home ;
Though fixed were my fate in the dark wave to perish,
    I would not besprinkle thy bower with foam.
When cold o'er my soul the black water was rushing,
    To gulf every hope once so verdantly bright,
As onward destroying, the flood-tide came gushing,
    My last look should be to thy haven of light.
Hung high in the air above mortals' rude grasping,
    Are lanterns festooning on China's glad fête ;
A sad child of poverty, breathless and gasping,
    One single lamp proffers, alas! all too late.
So he gazes in grief, on this bright scene of splendour,
    Yet he seeks not to dim one iota of blaze,
But he watches with care and solicitude tender,
    As he wanders away, yet looks back on the rays.

Oh, would that the thoughts that like Autumn leaves
    falling,
    Have withered and left me to mourn their decay,
Could come from Oblivion's dark cell at my calling,
    How gladly my spring-buds in homage I'd pay.
But think not if plague-spot of evil had tainted,
    One breath of contagion should light on thy shrine ;
Far less that thy faith, now so heavenly sainted,
    Should be stained with the doublings that struggled
    with mine.

A SEARCH AFTER HAPPINESS.

"O Happiness! our being's end and aim!
Good, pleasure, ease, content, whate'er thy name;
That something still which prompts th' eternal sigh,
For which we bear to live, or dare to die;
Which still so near us, yet beyond us lies;
O'erlooked, seen double, by the fool and wise;
Plant of celestial seed! if dropped below —
Say in what mortal soil thou deign'st to grow?"

POPE.

HAPPINESS! what art thou? The sought of many—
the obtained of none—the toy of our youth—the dream
of our age; ever near and never caught. Yet who can
hold thee fast, seeing we know thee not, nor where to
find thee? We ask thy dwelling and each points out a
varied road. "Seek her," say the young and elastic-
bounding, "seek her on the rosy lips, and the dimpled
cheek; she dwells in the liquid glance and the melting
clasp; her couch is on fragrant flowers, and her home
in the soul-drawn kiss." I sought her and I found her
not.

I asked of the warrior; and he bade me to the
clarioned field and the ensanguined moat. Was she in
the death-crowned breach? Chance, yes; but I heard
not her voice, for the wounded moaned too loudly. The
miser told me she was locked in his chest, but he would
not venture to open it, lest she should escape from him.
And the priest, he could not unclasp his breviary to aid
in his search, the leaves were clotted with some recu-
sant's blood. The monarch said 'twas in his crown;
but the crown shivered, and I saw its emptiness.

The mother pointed to her sleeping child; I looked again—it was in the sleep of eternity. She flitted awhile before applauded merit—a some-time guest with the sons of genius; but she fled as she heard the steps of poverty advancing.

Happiness! where, and in what clime dwellest thou? In the northern wilds—civilised Scythia—where mind and body alike are chilled? In Moslem-land? where the soul, like a crowded harem, is stored with beauteous images, yet only sensual in voluptuousness; surely not with thee. Art thou for Europe's grasp? Canst thou mingle in the motley group, where statesmen elbow statesmen, weaving chicanery; where the merchant gazes on the broad and heaving bosom of the sea—not to admire her beauties, but to think on the treasures she may bear to him; where virtue is recumbent, and mammon triumphant? Oh! not for thee, Europe! Bleeding Poland wails at the Russian despot; England, France, in their calculating policy, saw thee, unheeded, fall; · can they be happy with that remembrance?

Iberia! Lusitania! Hibernia! crouch in enslaving chains, or of superstition, or of tyranny; and bereaved and debased Italia, proud loved of Cybele—now the earth-trodden of the Austrian—with thee, with her— Oh, no!

Art thou happy, Greece—poets'-land—inspiration's birthplace—liberty's tomb? The bowstring scarce untwisted from thy neck, some rude Bavarian (thy Miltiades ne'er had known his country) lords it alike o'er Arcady and Boeotia, or the river Acheron, or the vale of Tempe.* Corinth! with Athens on the east,

* "Le temps a changé tout cela."

o

Sparta on the south; more immortalised still, with **Byron**
thy bard; how known now?   By a small round grape,
wherein thy very name, as if in shame, is emasculated.
Is this the happy land—the proud and the free?   Thy
some-time master, the Turkoman—connecting link, leads
me to Asiatic realms.   For happiness, shall I ask of the
beauty-gulfing Bosphorus tales of the Fanār; where
all the loveliest flowers are hived, encaged, till man
with ruthless hand shall come to gather; where lust is
dominant, and love—alas! where love is not, is not
happiness.   But I pass in fancy's flight near Nineveh,
and 'mid its ruins methought I saw that "woman-king,"
whose death was an atonement for his life; and he—he
seemed happy on the pyre his own " Ionian Myrrha "
had shared with him.   But it was delusion all. · Iran,
the glorious region, thy sun has set; thy Satraps crush
thee as of yore; not even in remembrance art thou joyful.
Happiness!   I catch the sound—and I fly o'er the flowering land, o'er the burning sand; alas "Felix" is no more
—Deserta remains.   Syria is desolate—I weep for the
woes of Palestine.   Hindustan tempts me, but Plutus fol-
lows in the track of Juggernaut, from Cashmere's lake
down to the plains of the Carnatic.   I could not enter into
the Celestial Empire, but I saw the pagod of Fohi in the
back-ground, and the little children floating dead on the
waves, while the mother sat listlessly on the banks, and
I said to myself, there is no happiness with the Tartar.

Away from Asia on imagination's car—as I pass, I
see the little lights glittering on the streams, amid those
spicy islets; and there were bright eyes watching those
love-freighted barks—those eyes spoke of Happiness;
a storm arose—the mimic fleet was scattered, and the
shore was deserted.

To Afric. To Mizräim—the eldest child of science—
the primogenitor of civilization—the nursling of old
philosophy. Hieroglyphic land! whose facts are as
romance and whose history of miracles. Ruled of the
priestcraft—of the Pharaoh—of her for whom the world
was well lost—of the Roman—of the Turk—of the
Idolater—and of the Moslem—land of the enslaving;
land of the enslaved! Terror-stricken by the wonders
of the "Passage," wert thou happy then? Soul-
bound by the mysteries of Eleusis, was Typhon a
comforter? Thy happiness, like thine own dead, was
enwrapt in enfolding bandages and in gilded gaudy
colourings. As at thine own feasts, still sat some
skeleton—an Actium to engulf thy silken-swelling sails;
an Acre to triumph over the darings of ambition. Now
thou art again civilised—thy Merchant-Pasha plants
olive-trees, and exports their oil; and thy warrior
Mamelukes, resting awhile from internal massacre,
watch o'er thy cargoes of cotton, or alike indifferent,
assist in transporting thy time-hallowed monuments.
Away from Egypt—once how superior! Giant cities—
Thebes and Hieropolis, and Memphis and Alexandria—
I may see you again in sadness—never in my search
for happiness! And where shall I rest on thy continent,
O Afric? I gaze around, and I see a burning and an
arid soil. Here, where man is sacrificed to savage
cruelty—there to more savage avarice. Round thy
coasts—those piratical hordes—all, all is ensanguined,
by blood—by crime.

I hear the language of my native land; I pause—
they read the funeral dirge over the last of five brothers.
I breathe but pestilence. Why came they there? I
wonder. I ask of some pallid and decrepid youth. He

points a little to the east, and there lie the Grain Coast, and the Ivory Coast, and the Gold Coast—I wonder no more.

From Guinea's Gulf, o'er the broad Atlantic, I haste, I haste. One moment on Helena's Isle; there I stand beneath the willow shade, and I commune with the mighty spirit—the fate-worker—Napoleon. I speak to him of happiness. I ask him of his school-boy days at Brienne's youthful college, when he strove ever to be foremost. He answers, ambition! I lead him to the hydra-headed monster, France's revolution. I place him at Toulon's breach; what impelled him there? Ambition. What led him o'er the bridge of Lodi? Ambition. He conquered the Austrian—he subjugated Italy—was he happy? He was ambitious. In Egypt, I spoke of Jaffa—and while he shuddered, I could not think of happiness. When at that famous council— where now at the dagger's point—now to dignity exalted—was he happy then? He was of the consuls— he was *the* consul—was he even then content? He, the unknown of Ajaccio, now the ruler of the people—no! no! he was still ambitious. Of St. Bernard's wondrous traversing—of his glorious warfare—of his more glorious peace—in all the commanding—the conquering— was he happy? No! no! no! still, still ambitious— the Imperial purple floated in the distant horizon—the crown of Charlemagne was in the o'erhanging expanse. The robes were donn'd—the iron crown himself had placed on his brow. "Vive l'Empereur!" shouted thousands of voices—millions of hearts re-echoed the cry. Then—then was he happy? Italy, Germany, Prussia, Spain, Europe! crouching at his feet; kings his vassals. Ambition's summit was reached; now the halcyon days were coming? No, he was childless. He had none born in his house to be his heir. His Josephine—she was happy in His glory—and he wept—aye, even Napoleon wept, as he remembered their parting. The proud house of Hapsburg wooed him in alliance, and Maria Louisa shared his couch—he became a father. Hope had pointed, and expectation was realised. Again I reiterated my question—if of man's desires all fulfilled, springs contentment? Faintly, but with a soldier's homage, he murmured "Spain," and I saw a noble hero rushing to wrest the laurel from his brow. I saw him, the fame-girt conqueror—the brave, the immortal Wellington.

Ambition was again afoot, and where she treads, contentment vanishes. With glowing breasts, and enraptured shouts the myriads entered Russia. And he, the chief—the idolised of all. He spoke of Smolensko and of Moscow. Still ambition led him on—now defeated—now retreating—still the glorious—still the Emperor. The Cossack was in Paris; and he a petty chieftain in the Isle of Elba. What awaited his return? Bosoms were bared to receive him. Was he happy? No! Paris was in the distance. The Tuileries were entered. With happiness? No! the vision answered, with ambition. The warrior at Waterloo—the captive in the Bellerophon—the exile at St. Helena; deprived, so ruthless policy dictated, of all those ties which might endear even exile; oh, was his death-bed happy? as I paused for the reply, some rude red-coated official warned me from the warrior's tomb.

Now to America, in imagination's search. Not in the icy regions would I commence; they were near to Europe. I asked in the States of Congress, but they

were too busy in their calculation of the value of slaves
in this land of liberty, to answer my enquiries, and I
saw in their election agitations that only in name were
they "United." A stalwart red-man lay across my path;
I thought from exhaustion, but saw it was intoxication.
I asked him were his fathers happy? A Kentuckian
boasted of having shot the last of the Fox-feet. Was he
happy? No! skins were at a discount. Almost in
despair, I sought in Mexico—when I asked for happiness, they showed me gold.

The bending cocoa, and the flowering aloe, and the
luscious pine, and the banana, and the fig and the
orange, and the thousand sweets of the Western Indies
lured me to the Tropics. I saw a bird of gaudy plu-
mage hover awhile o'er the lacerated back of some
mangled slave—there came a rush of wind, and that
bird, and that slave, lay with the scattered fruits,
beneath the blast of the tornado. In all the south of
this vast hemisphere, I saw alike superstitious credulity
and corrupting avarice—men, themselves slaves to
ignorance, fighting with cruel earnestness for a phantom
they called Liberty. Rapidly, like their own indigenous
thistles, which in one night spring to the height of
several feet, impeding civilisation and advancement; so
springing into note were petty chieftains, like these
thistles worthless; like them too, wounding and encum-
bering the land. Here I knew well happiness could
not abide.

I had heard of those isles of the Pacific, some
friendly in name, all of them in nature. One of them
I sought, and saw two missionary chapels and three
billiard rooms; on the shore, a native was extorting
some extra dollars for a heap of yams, which his father

would have been pleased to offer as a gift; while at his side were two angry disputants, debating the question, "whether the advancement of civilisation is conducive to happiness!"

My search is fruitless—in every age, in every clime, in every state, I have sought thee and found thee not. Art thou indeed of those things, which fancy visions, and which exist not in reality; with Dragons and with Griffins, and the Phœnix and the Kraken? or if thou do exist, under such varied forms we know thee not, nor where to seek thee. Undefinable Proteus—vision—cheat—shadow—phantom—Happiness!

THE SINNER AND THE BIBLE.

תשב אנוש עד דכה ותאמר שובו בני אדם
תהלים צ"ג'

"Thou bringest man to contrition, and sayest, Repent ye sons of man."
PSALM XC. 3.

"Bless'd tears of soul-felt penitence,
  In whose benign, redeeming flow,
Is felt the first, the only sense,
  Of guiltless joy, that guilt can know." MOORE.

WET with many tears,
The Bible lay before him;
  Wet with many tears,
  For wither'd hopes and wasted years,
  Grief-stain'd the sacred page appears,
  When memory's mournful pall uprears,
And buried shades flit o'er him.

Wet with tears of shame,
God's words his deeds reproaching;
  Wet with tears of shame,
    For life of ill-dishonour'd name,
    For powers misused and blighted fame;
    Thus wakened thoughts his acts proclaim,
God's book with fear approaching.

  Wet with tears of dread,
Of guilt the doom appalling;
  Wet with tears of dread,
    His burning eyes have woe-full read,
    How surely sin to sorrow led;
    Remorse doth molten tear-drops shed,
Thick rain from dark clouds falling.

  Wet with tears of hope,
"Turn from evil ways and live;"
  Wet with tears of hope,
    As out at sea the telescope,
    (While yet 'mid gloom the seamen grope)
    Foreshows where dawn and daylight ope,
"Father," he cries "forgive."

  Wet with tears of joy,
See! mercy yet in heaven;
  Wet with tears of joy,
    No more earth-soiling passions cloy,
    New hopes his racking cares destroy;
    He feels a bliss without alloy,
Contrite—his sins forgiven.

" OF MAN'S FIRST DISOBEDIENCE."

A RABBINICAL TRADITION.

Eve ate the fatal fruit—self-doomed, said Adam, "Give,
With thee to share and die; alone 'twere death to live."

תהלה לאל עליון

PRAISE TO THE MOST HIGH.

A PARAPHRASE OF נשמת כל חי

Sabbath Morning Service.

The breath of all that lives shall praise Thy name,
The spirit of all flesh Thy might proclaim ;
With loftiest strains extolling, ceaseless sing,
Memorials grateful of the Eternal King.
Where myriad worlds thro' endless space outshine,
Protector, Saviour, God, in Thee combine.
When care or sorrow clouds the anxious brow,
Our sole Redeemer, sole Protector, Thou !
From earliest date, to final doom unchanged,
Unchecked, Thy power o'er boundless time hath ranged.
Creation's Lord ! see all creation's ranks,
Extol Thy Name in amplitude of thanks.
In mercy He His world with kindness leads,
With tender care His creatures' wants still heeds.
Nor sleepeth He—nor seeks to slumber—God ;
Who sleep, He wakens, rouseth whoso nod ;

The dumb thro' Him in eloquence outpour,
And slaves in freedom joy—bound now no more;
Sustained who droop, upraised the fallen, now,
To Thee, O God, to Thee alone we bow.

If filled our mouths (as teems the sea) with song,
Fluent our tongues, as roll swift waves along;
Our lips replete—our raptured eyes intent,
As gleam bright orbs in Thine own firmament;
Heavenwards (like eagles) hands outstretched in prayer,
Fleet in good paths our feet like hinds' feet were;
Our best attempts e'en then were idly weak,
Thy Name to bless, Thy boundless praise to speak.
Yea! e'en for one, of thousand mercies wrought,
Or myriad bounties yielded e'en unsought,
Or marvels Thine, Thou didst our fathers show,
Or wondrous kindness we their children know.
From Egypt's land redeemed, O God, by Thee;
From slavery's bonds by Thy dread power set free;
In famine fed, from plenty's bounteous store;
From ruthless sword, from sickness fell and sore,
From withering plagues, from all of pain or ill,
Released, unharmed, by Thine Almighty will;
Protected yet, in mercy prone to spare;
So ne'er forsaken, still we own Thy care.

Each pulse for this, each nerve, each quick'ning sense,
The breath Thou gavest—soul Thou didst dispense,
Volition, motion, speech, shall all combine,
To hail their Author—glorious, great, divine!
To bless, to praise, to glorify Thy Name;
Thy might, dominion, sanctity, proclaim;

Each mouth adoring offers Thee its prayer,
Each tongue, in truth, to Thee alone shall swear,
To Thee each knee its grateful homage lend,
And all that lives, in reverence shall bend.
Imbued with awe, shall thrill each conscious heart,
With joy exult each vein, each inward part;
So wrote the bard "my essence all shall speak,
Who equals God that guards the poor and weak,
Releasing him where tyrants harshly press,
And rescuing safe from harm and dire distress?"

Who like to Thee? In aught who can array?
Comparison with Thee, what being dare essay?
Thou great, tremendous, mighty, awful Lord!
In Heaven obeyed, alike on earth adored.
And so Thy worth, tho' feebly, we confess,
Still shall we praise, still glorify, still bless;
"Bless God," so David sang, "so thou, my soul, exclaim,
So shall my heart and inmost soul adore His Holy
    Name."

PSALM XXIV.

Earth unto the Lord belongs,
    King! he o'er its fulness reigns;
Worlds amid their dwellers' throngs,
    Own that to Him all pertains.

Based upon the depthless seas,
    Fixed by His Almighty power,
'Stablished there by God's decrees,
    Firm 'mid floods does earth uptower.

Who to God's high hill shall mount?
    Who his course shall thither tend?
Holy praises to recount,
    Who to Holy place ascend?

Hands—spot-free from vice or sin,
    Heart—ne'er stained with guilt impure,
Soul—vain thoughts ne'er entered in,
    Lips—whose words as oaths are sure.

This the man, the Lord who loves;
    Blessings He for such receives;
Righteousness;—whom God approves,
    Gifted with salvation lives.

Sacred race, who truthful speak,
    Here their just ensemblance view;
Pure in heart, the Lord who seek,
    Still they Jacob's God will sue.

High! ye gates! your heads uprise,
    E'er-enduring doors ope wide;
Comes the Lord of earth and skies,
    Glory's King—the heaven's pride.

Glory's King, bedecked in light;
    Who is this that hither tends?
He, the potent, strong in fight,
    God, the mighty, hither wends.

High! ye gates! your heads uprise,
    E'er-enduring doors ope wide,
Comes the Lord of earth and skies,
    Glory's King—the heaven's pride.

"Glory's king bedecked in light,"
  Who this honoured title boasts?
Who?—The potent, strong in fight,—
  Glory's king—the God of Hosts.

LIFE.

FOUR PICTURES.

I.

O BEAUTEOUS child! O vision bright as fair!
What sparkling eyes; what clustering auburn hair;
What roseate charms bedeck each dimpled cheek,
And lips though mute, most eloquent which speak.
A lovely form, wherein enrapt we trace,
The embryo blossoms of each freshening grace;
And Time's each hour, a life of bliss foretelling,
Sheds light and lustre o'er thy favoured dwelling.

II.

Another form:—still lovely in the change;—
As o'er some bright parterre in spring we range,
And soft Creation cheers our gladdened view,
With graceful bud and tints of varied hue;
And when we tread again that verdant vale,
Odŏrous* sweets the fragrant flowers exhale;
So, wreaths of Love and fruits of Hope entwining,
Bright Summer's sunlight still is o'er thee shining.

* "The bright consummate flower
  Spirits odŏrous breathes."
        MILTON. *Paradise Lost*, v. 482.

ʻIII

Again we view : now round thy ripened bloom,
What new-born graces multiplied resume ;
As when some Indian tree that bends to earth,
Its shoots upspring in emulative birth ;
Repeated there the parent's gifts combine,
Round kindred mother, graceful offspring twine ;
Still beauty o'er thy mellowed charms pervading,
And e'en more beauteous in this lovely shading.

IV.

And yet again.—But see that withered crone,
Mocking she gibes, and speaks in mournful tone—
" ' O beauteous child ! O vision bright as fair ! '
Look at my wasted cheeks, my time-bleached hair.
' Another form :—still lovely in the change,'
O'er palsied limbs let now thine eyelids range.
' Again we view, now round thy ripened bloom,'
My hopes, my children, wither in the tomb."

THE CREED

(BEING A PARAPHRASE OF THE HYMN יגדל אלי׳ חי).

EXTOL we now the living God,
　　His praises loud relate,
Who is, and whose existence is
　　Nor bound by time or date.

Who, One and only One alone,
　　Invisible doth dwell ;
And peerless in His Unity,
　　His limit who shall tell.

Material form, similitude,
  Or likeness none hath He ;
Nor can there to His Holiness,
  Comparison e'er be.

Ere glad Creation at His word
  To life and light outburst ;
Of primal date—Eternal He,
  Without beginning, First.

Of all the Lord ; the wide expanse,
  Its dwellers all around,
Proclaim His might, His majesty,
  Which everywhere abound.

Prophetic powers he deigned to grant,
  Blessed words of Revelation,
To them, His treasured men of worth,
  In glorious inspiration.

But like to Moses none arose,
  'Mid Israel's chosen few,
Who face to face with God did speak,
  And did His semblance view.

And when, in mercy, laws of truth,
  God for His people penned,
He by that faithful prophet pleased,
  His holy law to send.

Nor ever will our gracious Lord,
  Another code bestow ;
For, all complete, His perfect law
  No altering change can know.

Our hidden thoughts, our every act,
    From Him are ne'er concealed;
Yea! ere commenced, of all the end
    To Him at once revealed.

Rewarding kindness as his due;
    The good man's just return;
But to the wicked, punishment,
    His own misdoings earn.

Who at His time—in length of days,
    Will our Messiah send;
Redeeming those who anxious wait
    Salvation as their end.

In wondrous mercy, then, the dead
    Revive at God's behest;
Be then His praises ever sung,
    His name be ever blest.

THREE DREAMS.

I.

I DREAMED I was in heaven. Centered there
Was store of valued wealth beyond compare;
Inestimable heaps—gems of countless price,
The miser's mind insatiate might suffice;
Gold, diamonds, pearls, mystic ocean's treasure;
Ministring unscant, limitless in measure;
And men and women, pleased in this possessing,
Feeding in pomp, nor seeking other blessing;

Gorgeous-arrayed in richest robes of state,
Prompt at their beck dependent flatterers wait;
How rich! how grand! how lofty! and how proud!
As wit and wisdom at their biddings bowed;
And beauty too, resplendent to behold,
All else subduing, owns the might of gold;
With glittering chains the wreaths of love entwined,
And gold enthralled the universal mind;
Careless of future, reckless of the past,
Thoughtless of present, so these bright hours last,
Glorying in riches, rank, and pride of birth;
I dreamed I was in heaven; I woke—'twas earth.

II.

I dreamed I was in heaven. The morning hour,
Waking, renewed, each dewy-spangled flower;
In thrilling tones the raptured feathered throng;
Carolled melodious their skilled untutored song;
A fragrant dell, where sheltered all around,
The homes of happiness gracefully abound;
Hopeful, content, was heard their gladsome voice,
Whose guileless hearts in virtuous deeds rejoice;
This pleasant scene the sun's bright beams disclose,
Lovely and tranquil, calm in blessed repose.
A sound discordant grates the affrighted ear,
As troops infuriate o'er the hills appear,
Trampling their fierce steeds 'cross the flowery heath,
Hurling their blood-brands, woman's breast the sheath,
Burning, destroying, merciless, each home,
Driving the houseless babes, orphans to roam;
In sacred fanes, o'er murdered priests who trod,
Kneeling in blasphemy, thank Eternal God;

D

While mumbled prayers commix with drunken yell;
I dreamed I was in heaven—alas! 'twas hell!

III.

I dreamed I was in heaven.   Stillness and night,
Not dark, but radiant in celestial light;
Various the scenes that met my wondering gaze,
Of worth and valour, shrinking back from praise;
Of patriot courage, nerved with iron-like will,
Patient, oft downcast, but triumphant still;
Of filial love, tuning a sweet old rhyme,
That quick recalls the old man's youthful prime;
Of fond affection, two as one combined,
Where heart with heart, and love with love was twined;
Of gentle pity yielding home and rest,
To soothe and calm the fever'd anguish'd breast;
Of reverend age with fervent honest zeal,
The mind to cure, the wounded soul to heal.
All this I viewed with raptured sense and sight,
While radiant-beaming shone that living light,
And sweet rich voices floated through the air,
Harmonious age with feeble child at prayer;
Entranced I saw thus good to good succeed;
I dreamed I was in heaven—'twas heaven indeed!

——o——

THE SPIRIT OF ELIJAH.

הנה אנכי שלח לכם את אליה הנביא

מלאכי ג" כג'

"Behold I send unto you Elijah the prophet." MALACHI, iii. 23.

"Open the door."—See *Passover Evening Service.*

To think! that spirits good and pure,
    Invisible do roam,
From guile and sin our hearts to cure,
    And sanctify our home.
To think! the prophet, God inspired,
    Immortal life who won,
Again, with holy ardour fired,
    A mortal's course doth run.

To think! on each recurring year,
    Earth's paths again to press,
His spirit leaves its heavenly sphere,
    Our meal and oil to bless; *
To whisper comfort to the sad,
    Bright hope Elijah giveth;
'Mid lone grief bids the heart be glad,
    "For see your dear child liveth." †

To think! again with zeal impressed,
    Sin's altars crushed to break, ‡
He comes, God's messenger confessed,
    Our sleeping thoughts to wake.

* 1 Kings xvii. 16.   † Ibid. xvii. 23.   ‡ Ibid. xviii. 21, etc.

To show, forewarn'd the awful day,
    The "still small voice" bid hear; *
To tell, though past from mortal sway,
    His watchful form is near.

It needs no stretch of fancy's dreams,
    These thoughts to realise ;
Where light religion's soul-fed beams,
    Elijah's footstep hies.
With welcome, haste—with joy replete,
    "Make pure thy path before,"
For they who would good spirits greet,
    Themselves must "ope the door."

TO JESSY.

(WITH A BOUQUET OF FLOWERS.)

THOUGH some may prize the fragrant rose,
    Whilst others for the lily pine,
Yet still I'd value more than those,
    To have the lovely Jessy-mine.

HABITS OF HOLINESS.

(AN EPIGRAM.)

"THY priests shall clothe in righteousness,"
    Thus sacred precepts say ;
But Nadab wears not, you may guess,
    His best clothes every day.

* 1 Kings xix. 12.

THE LITTLE FRENCH MILLINER.

A TALE OF THE PAST.

I WAS in the habit of passing my college vacations
principally with a good-natured uncle, who lived a life
of ease and comfort, at his country mansion in one of
the Midland districts. I am not about to describe his
dwelling, more than to mention that it was perfect in
all that could conduce to convenience and enjoyment.
Uncle Edward was particularly solicitous to contribute
in every way to our entertainment; and when the
weather prevented our partaking in any out-door
athletic sports, he would beguile, with tales of adventure, hours which might otherwise have been wearisome. One narrative specially interested us, though
there was nothing important about it—yet somehow it
so fixed itself on my memory (for Uncle Edward often
"spoke like a book") that I think I can almost remember his very words, which ran thus—speaking of his
own youth :

Monsieur, as we called our French master at
Bedford, was one of those peculiar characters, that
stamp themselves in originality on the young mind.
What he had been, previous to his coming to our
school, we could not guess; some said a nobleman;
others, with equal probability, a perruquier. One, who
had seen him carefully brightening a rusted rapier,
which hung in useless inactivity in his chamber, pro-
nounced him a *ci-devant militaire;* another, who had
watched his eager gaze at some faded rose-colour
ribbons, set him down as a man-milliner. Enquiries
on the subject he evaded, sometimes with a smile—

often with a sigh. However, whatever he had been, he was esteemed by us all; even Big Burnet, the bully of the boys, and the plague of the ushers, spared him from molestation. Neat in his attire, unaffected in manner, and assiduous in his duties, when school-hours were over, he would read to a willing auditory, legends of the historian, Alain Chartier, or wondrous deeds of chivalry out of Froissart or Monstrelet, when his eye would gleam with a fire very different from his wonted placidity. Sometimes he would, with a skilful hand, accompany himself on the guitar, in some old Provençal melody, or lay of the wandering Troubadour, so sweetly, that even "Sour Sarah," as the boys used to call the housekeeper, came out of the pantry to listen to him.

Toujours gai! was his motto—only on the mournful anniversaries of his sovereign's martyrdom would he confine himself to solitude. "*Toujours gai,*" as I have said, as the odour of the musk plant sheds its fragrance on all within its reach, so did his exuberance of spirits diffuse a pleasurable sensation over his associates. But on Saturday evenings he was always particularly mirthful; then would he laugh the merriest, and his little silken skirted coat would wag responsive to his exhila-rated movements; on Saturday evenings his daughter would call to visit him, and frequently would her entreaties win him home to her humble lodgings on the Sunday. Right eagerly would these hebdomadal visits be anticipated, and joyously would he spring to the hall door to clasp his sole remaining life prop, his beloved Adeline.

The sweetest girl I ever knew was Adeline, and as she tripped across the play-ground, clinging to the arm of her delighted father, there was scarcely a boy

that did not leave his sport and come with a word of
greeting to Mademoiselle. I can but just remember
her glance; so mild, that it would seem to encourage
the most timid, yet with such a lurking fire in her eyes
that the boldest might be daunted. Moving more with
the gracefulness of a sylph than the pertness of a gri-
sette, the springing lightness of her petite form bounded
on in all the elasticity of youth and innocence. A little
basket, tastefully decorated, contained her weekly presents to her father, and the most handsome bouquet of
the season was always brought for his acceptance. A
love of flowers, as a fair and valued friend observed to
me, is always a proof of a susceptible mind, and I
conceived a more favourable opinion of Adeline from
her fondness for these, earth's loveliest children. Yet
those who knew her station, which was only that of
assistant to a neighbouring village dressmaker, could
not conceive how she could contrive to procure such
beautiful exotics, the purchase of which must have been
far beyond her means. Some did say, that the camelias
were very much like those in the Grange, and the
Squire's daughters did not scruple to toss their heads,
and wonder why Mr. George would cut so many of his
finest geraniums for a little French milliner, when he
had refused them only a sprig the day before.

Well! it was so—Monsieur kissed her as they parted
at the gate, and did not object to confide her to the care
of the young candidate for holy orders, who was over
ready to escort her to her home. They waited but his
induction to a promised living for the good old French-
man to consent to their union. Daily did our regard
for Monsieur increase, so kind was he to all; content
with his lot, even out of his trifling pittance he con-

trived to afford assistance to his less fortunate countrymen. In fact, if ever man seemed divested of evil
passions, it was our Gallic friend; and his little smiling
daughter, partaking of all her father's good qualities,
was a general favourite, not only with us, but with all
who knew her. She had gradually established a small
connection in the village, and many a blushing country
maid was now attired with a degree of taste and neat-
ness which rendered them doubly attractive in the eyes
of their wondering Cymons.

I removed from school, and in advancing adolescence
and London gaieties forgot youth's reminiscences. I
had rambled into "Offley's" one night, to take a
glass of wine and a cigar, after my return from the
theatre; but perhaps I had better first describe
what I mean by "Offley's."* Not far from the
theatres, suppose a tavern whose hospitable doors are
open to receive the welcome guest, even at an hour
when the more quiet citizens have soberly gone to rest.
If, wearied with the monotony of a modern drama, you
long for more refreshing diet, or if with prudent prospec-
tive, you think of the empty larder and the crabbed land-
lady at home—if the night air nips you—if the evening at
Mrs.——'s has been more than usually dull, (perhaps
because her daughters have laboured to be more than
usually lively), if you are out of spirits—if you are in
spirits—in short, "be thy intent wicked or charitable," if
to pass an hour of the midnight morning in enjoyment be
your object, go at once to Offley's. At tables, placed on
either side of a long room on the first floor, are groups,
laughing, chatting and joking; cheating the night's

* Now a thing of the past.

tediousness with their merriment. Foaming ale, which might tempt Bacchus from his wine-cup, and still replenished goblets of every varied cordial compound, are lavished round with no unsparing hand; busily employed waiters are bustling to and fro, with a constant supply of humble though substantial fare; and where the eye can pierce through the fumes of the Virginian weed, you see all around making desperate havoc with the provender. Now there's a whisper—a buzz of excitement—who is it? Mr. Mordaunt Granville St. Clair, (the pleasant rogues have all such grandiloquent names) the gentleman whom you remember as the second robber in the Miller and his Men; and his chivalrous-looking companion, is the gifted demon of the Drury Lane establishment. The arrival of these Roscii causes quite a sensation. Now with shouts uproarious a song is loudly called for; "the Captain" takes the chair, and anacreontics and comicalities, war songs and erotics, follow each other in quick confusion. A tolerably executed glee, in which the histrionic gentleman with the euphonious cognomen takes the falsetto, thereby earning his nightly modicum, excites peals of applause from would-be musical amateurs.

> "Mirth and fun grow fast and furious."

The cares of the day are forgotten, and now alive are

> "Jest and youthful jollity,
> Quips and cranks, and wanton wiles,
> Nods and becks, and wreathed smiles,
> Sport that wrinkled Care derides,
> And Laughter holding both his sides."

I noticed at a side table, rather apart from the boisterous merriment, a young man, clad in rusty black, who, as if ashamed of being seen, had withdrawn himself from publicity, as not wishing to partake in the general enjoyment. His single glass, oft diluted, served as an excuse for his protracted stay, even until the first dawn of light, which now came peeping through the window shutters, like a sly girl, who, while she covers her eyes with her hands, looks through the interstices of her fingers at some favoured lover she delights to tease. Changeful, as the same coquette, who has helped me to this simile, the sun had hardly wakened to usher in a bright May morning, when the native fickleness of England's clime interposed a thickened veil of intercepting clouds, and a heavy shower began to descend. The young man, who had risen to depart, seemed annoyed at this, and resumed his seat with evident unwillingness. Seeing his uneasiness, and the waiter having now brought me an umbrella, I offered to share it with the stranger; this offer he accepted with thanks, and our routes being similar, we entered into conversation, which was deeply interesting to me, being stored with intelligence and information on his part, that imparted a value even to common-place subjects, as at the touch of the Phrygian king the baser metals turned to gold.

A casual allusion to Bedford, induced a start on the part of my companion, and a consequent remark caused me to recognise in my new found acquaintance, George Wilton of the Grange, and the remembered suitor of the little French milliner. Arriving at my lodgings, I requested his company to breakfast, of which he having partaken with an avidity that excited his own observation and apology, I asked him news of our old friend Monsieur and his pretty daughter. Sighing deeply, he told me that his father having discovered his attachment for Adeline, and being irritated by its determined continuance, the Grange was no longer a home for him. So far did the old man carry his resentment as to prevail on his patron to revoke the promised living. "I was therefore," said he, "almost destitute; but cheered by the smiles of my dear girl and the continued encouragement of her father, I did not despair. Blessed with some talents, I determined to exert them, and after an affectionate farewell with my friends, set out for London. This was the last time I ever saw them.

"The overthrow of Napoleon recalled the Bourbons, and their partisans hastened to Paris. The rusted rapier was withdrawn from useless inactivity and restored to pristine brightness, to glitter by the side of the last of the De Guesclins. Not more rapid than had been the alteration in his circumstances, was the change in the character of the now ennobled Count from the humble teacher. All the latent passions which had for years lain dormant, now sprang up with added strength, as the earth-hidden dragon teeth grew into armed men;* pride, ambition, arrogance, and self-love, qualities one would little have thought lurking under his placid demeanor, now, like serpents warmed from torpidity, ruled with re-asserted venom power. The first exertion of his authority was a command never again to see me; on her remonstrances, he, now supplied with ample resources, hurried her to France, and our last communication was a brief but

* "Vipereos dentes, populi incrementa futuri."

love-breathing letter ere her departure. Since then I have never heard of her; doubtless she has forgotten me—time has passed, 'Tempus edax rerum.'

"So have I struggled on, supporting myself by literary contributions, one of the 'genus irritabile'; at length the productions on which I was engaged failed, and the abstruse studies to which I had devoted myself were less pleasing to the gentle public, than the fanciful puerilities of ephemeral novels; to this I never could apply myself, and I have often shared the fate of wiser and better men—starvation. Sometimes I have earned a temporary respite by translations for some speculative booksellers; last evening the purpose of my visit to a place so little congenial to my feelings, was a promised interview with a flighty young bibliopolist, who forsooth, had, in his whimsical caprice, appointed a midnight tavern meeting, as a fitting occasion to discuss a purposed version of Theocritus. The inconsiderateness that would appoint such a meeting had little scruple in disappointing a poor author, and I lingered with hope deferred, till warning note of time forbade me prospect of ingress at my humble lodgings."

"It is hardly worth boasting," continued Uncle Edward "that I enabled him to obtain a permanent livelihood; much of my little classic lore do I owe to the superior attainments of my talented friend. We were walking together down Oxford Street, when the sight of a very pretty figure induced me to call his attention to its fair owner. With a cry of joy he discovered in the little French milliner before us his own Adeline. The father, now installed in one of the highest offices at the Court of the Tuileries, had, with increasing pride very different from his former comportment, interdicted all thoughts of her heart's treasurings; her letters, his letters had been intercepted; she had been led to consider him faithless; the death-bed of a domestic revealed the practised treachery, and in disgust she left her home for England. Enquiries at the Grange were met with denial and contumely. Indignant at the deception, she would not return to paternal grandeur, but preferred independence in the exertion of her graceful skill, and in the exciting hope of again encountering her unforgotten. One minute's interview, and they were again the loving—the beloved.

" This was about the time of the late king's accession, and France, as all other countries, sent gratulatory missions. To decorate the elegant tournure of the gay Duchesse de D—— who did the honours of the embassy, all the establishment of the talented Dévy were in requisition ; most pleasing of all were the attentions of a little French milliner, and she was specially invited, to the envy of her companions, to assist in attiring the swan-like beauty on the morning of the coronation. A light step, and a well-turned compliment ushered to the toilette the nobleman who was to be her escort to the pageant. Adeline started, the recognition was immediate ; and the father and daughter were locked in each other's arms."

" Well, Uncle," said we all eagerly, seeing he paused, " of course she was married to George." "Yes! my dears, she was ; last year I dined with the happy couple at their Bel-bois de Guesculin, and while their daughter Georgette, and her now smiling grandsire toyed in mutual gratification, we filled our Champagne d' Ai 'to the olden days at Bedford,' and the remembrance of the 'little French milliner.'"

FLIRTILLA.

(AN EPIGRAM.)

AT seventeen, Flirtilla cried,
I will not be Avaro's bride;
I scorn his proffers, spurn his gold,
I am too young,—he is too old.

At eighteen, and at twenty, too,
In vain she heard him vows renew;
In vain his love he still confess'd,
She still his anxious hopes repress'd.

At length his suit her swain forbore,
The proud Flirtilla's young no more;
Decays her beauty—fades her bloom;
With joy she weds Avaro's groom.

——o——

שתלי זתים

"OLIVE PLANTS."

A SACRED ENIGMA.

1. WEEPING, a mother saw her first-born slain;
   Another son! her hopes revive again.
2. 'Mid toil and trouble, hear the sire exclaim,
   "Comfort he gives," be "Comfort" then his name.
3. Hopeless in age, the matron sad behold—
   Radiant in smiles, her arms her child enfold.

4. Sweet infant buds the captive exile's balm,
   Whose "fruitful boughs" affliction's woes becalm.

5. With beating heart beside the sedgy Nile,
   She lays the cradled babe—ah! woe the while!
   But oh! what joy her raptured soul possessed—
   He draws the life-spring from his mother's breast.

6. That child a man, of two the happy sire,
   The "Help of God" doth "alien strange" desire.

7. "Barren and bearing not" shalt yet conceive,
   Whose wondrous strength Philistia's host shall
   grieve.

8. The youthful babe by "pleasant" grand-dam
   nurs'd,
   Whose after grandchild's heavenly hymns outburst.

9. Plaintive her heart—no voice the still air stirred;
   Yet see the boy, whose mother's prayer is heard.

10. Poor helpless widow,—lost her only one;
    The prophet cheers, "embrace thy living son."

11. And mighty she, yet poor, 'mid all her store,
    Whose child sore-stricken glads her eye no more;
    O marvel! joy! what new-born hopes upspring,
    In fond embraces child and mother cling.

——o——

But pause we here, though scripture leaves enshrine,
Long lists of loved ones—heritage divine.

12. One—Judah's king, that holy youth shall close,
    As then so now—may Israel find repose.

——o——

THE POWER OF GOOD.

TO ———.

WHERE thou art, there, no darkness is, for blessèd by
the ray
That beams from thine effulgent eye, the night seems
changed to day;
All nature brightly lives again, and wondering she
perceives
New light and lustre streaming forth: new life each
thing receives.
The bird that hears thy thrilling voice, grows envious
of the note,
And strains then most melodiously his music-warbling
throat;
In vain essays to catch the tone, the magic of thy voice,
That adds to every joy a bliss, that bids e'en grief
rejoice;
Above, around, on every side, admiring nature greets
Thy coming, robed in gentleness, and redolent of
sweets;
Odōrous flowers and fragrant herbs, had closed their
buds for night,
Thy presence quick unfolds their leaves, at new-created
light.

What varied sweets the emulous plants now raptur-
ously exhale,
Unconscious, vying with thy breath, the choicest scents
must fail,

Expanding at thy sun-like glance, each brightly gorgeous flower
Would proudly offer to our gaze its jewel-sparkled
dower ;
Yet vainly then awakened there, each richly teeming
grace,
We turn from their most lovely charms to thy more
lovely face ;
And though in them rich beauties rare to tempt our gaze
we find,
All these we find, and more in thee—in thee there lives
a mind ;
A mind imbued with loveliness, a pure clear radiance
bright,
That warms us with its cheering glow, that glads us
with its light.

The raging tempest stirs the deep, the forest quakes
with fear,
Affrighted hinds, in secret copse, the piercing lightnings
sear ;
Obscured and gloomed, and shrunk with awe, creation
seems to quail,
And wild turmoil runs riot now, 'mid fire and storm and
hail ;
Yet through this war of elements, like to some twinkling
star,
A little speck of blue outpeers, it glistens, there, afar ;
Out, out at sea—a hand's-breadth now, the horizon
fondly shrines
That speck of blue—it now expands ; celestial heaven
shines ;

E

Still'd at a breath, the tempest's rage, the forest-trees
 uprear,
And glittering drops on dancing sprays, proclaim a
 truce to fear ;
All, all is joy and happiness, glad smiles bedeck each
 cheek,
(Though nestling close, pretending fear, those tender
 lovers speak)
Outshines again the glorious orb, and springing back to
 life,
Where late was dread, now blossoms hope—and calmness, where was strife.

Thou camest—where souls in wild turmoil, with angry
 passions tost,
Prostrate, uptorn, each hope of life, gone—withered—
 wasted—lost !
Like lightning-blast, despair had scathed, the buds of
 early youth,
Torn, prone to earth lay scatter'd there, hope, faith, and
 love, and truth ;
One look—thine own—thy hand outstretched, and
 magic ! at thy spell,
Life's sap quick filled each wasted branch, the withered
 trunks outswell ;
A balm of peace is sprinkled o'er, and bud, and blos-
 som, leaf,
And trees of life and wisdom blend, where late was woe
 and grief.

Where foul miasma loads the air, and sinking nature
 faints,
Beneath the rank pestiferous cloud, the heavy air that
 taints ;

Sinking while all of living form, with tottering footsteps
    creep,
And vegetation lingering droops, in dull and heavy
    sleep;
No sound is heard to glad the ear, no sight to please
    the eye;
Where once to breathe, is doom to fade, where once to
    live, to die.
With godlike skill see science come, and from that rank
    impure,
Far fly away the poisonous damps, the cattle range
    secure,
Emerges many a teeming crop, that gilds the burdened
    land,
And clustering fruit now fill the bowl, by fragrant
    zephyrs fann'd;
Loud gladsome mirth, and laughing glee, now dance in
    myrtle shade,
Or listen to the warbled notes that thro' the air pervade:
E'en so thy words, like science—art, a gift from realms
    above,
Shed round their healing sanctity, and wake to life and
    love.

O! who can say? does Heaven's grace a foretaste send
    to earth,
To teach men how to reverence a form of heavenly
    birth!
That we might see and learn to love, those deeds of high
    emprize,
Should earn us right to dwell with Thee, in yonder
    gleaming skies.

Association with the good can win the doubting mind,
To rouse from dreamy apathy and fellow with his kind;
To quit the dull lethargic trance in which he power-
    less lies,
And won by virtue, good to love, with good to sympa-
    thise.

——o——

THE FISHERMAN.

A TALE, ADDRESSED TO THE LADIES.

A FISHERMAN, whose nets were new,
And every bait could bring in view;
Capricious as he plied his trade,
(Like many a young coquettish maid),
And all his prey rose to his wish,
Discarded many a useful fish;
But for a fancied fault, forsooth!
They did not please this squeamish youth.
Too large, too small, too thick, too thin,
Too dark a scale, too bright a fin;
Some reason, just as wise as these,
Would guide his purpose o'er the seas.
Yet once he said—to please his mind,
Some gold and silver fish he'd find;
He threw the net—the prey he sought;
They, not unwilling to be caught,
Came flocking fast in shoals to hand,
Yet scorned he now the glittering band;

For still he paused to scrutinize,
Imagined faults in shape or size;
And while he thus the time delays,
They're far beyond his listless gaze;
What cared he then the giddy youth,
He little needed them, in truth;
For now the river, brook, or seas,
Will yield their treasures at his ease;
He fishes now but to amuse,
He need but only pick and choose;
And soon his daily sport is done,
His nets are hanging in the sun.

But now! the voice of hunger speaks,
Again the rod and line he seeks;
Again essays the venturous trade;
Not as of yore his toil repaid;
The useful nets so long abused,
Or only sought to be misused,
No longer yield their wonted prey,
And why? They've fallen to decay.
The fisher views with sad alarm,
The progress of each direful harm;
The tattered mesh, the wasted twine,
And plies again the rod and line;
In vain his hook again he baits,
No finny spoil his longing sates;
In vain he plies each varied art,
Longs for the prey he sees depart;
Would fain his former hours retrace,
When master o'er the watery race,
He then could please each springing wish,
With choicest store of dainty fish;

And now, the meanest one of these,
Would he with joyful rapture seize,
Till fast receding day and light,
Compelled to quit his toil by night,
And homewards as he bends his way,
Sighs, "He that will not when he may,
When he will, he shall have nay."

———o———

THE PILGRIMS.

TO———.

ENTHUSIASTIC in their zeal,
   They traverse wild and waste;
And armed with holy purpose feel,
   More purified, more chaste;
As wending on their desort way,
   They near that sacred fane,
And votive heart-strains loudly say,
   " They have not toiled in vain."

Now home returned with joy elate,
   All worldly passions stilled,
In peaceful, blest and happy state,
   Life's holiest wish fulfilled.
The hallowed pilgrims thus we trace,
   Themselves of sacred worth;
Who once have reached that sainted place,
   Are sanctified thenceforth.

So, long through desert tracks my view,
   My faltering steps have sought,
That shrine my spirit might renew,
   With fresh created thought.
The mirage tempting in its green,
   Oft lured me with its cheat,
And where the sands shone liquid sheen,
   Illusions led my feet.

But now! joy-filled, I see enshrined,
   All e'er I hoped to see;
And God's own temple in thy mind,
   Hath bent my heart and knee.
New feelings in my soul abound,
   New virtues seem to woo;
Thus when we tread on holy ground,
   Ourselves turn holy too.

———o———

WHO IS MY NEIGHBOUR?

(AN EPIGRAM.)

To love thy neighbour as thyself,
   Is maxim good and true;
But you, who come to ask my pelf,
   It don't apply to you.

If love I to my "neighbour" give,
   In it have you no share;
For I in famed Belgravia live,
   And you in Goulston Square.

PSALM CXLVIII.

(PARAPHRASED.)

THROUGH earth, through air, through rolling sea,
Where'er Creation's forms there be ;
Where'er o'er space His power abounds,
Through myriad spheres His praise resounds.

Where ministering angels gladsome dwell,
Loud joyous notes of praise outswell ;
Where heavenly hosts in brightness shine,
Praiseful they tell His power divine.

The lucent moon, the stars at night,
The radiant sun in splendour dight,
The depths below, the heavens above,
Proclaim the God of truth and love.

He spoke—they shone—He willed—they stood,
Eternal fixed, and aye for good ;
They creatures of Almighty will,
Unchanged His purpose e'er fulfil.

Where raging tempests stir the deep,
Where wondrous forms through waves upleap,
'Mid fire and snow and hail are heard,
Obedient heralds of His word.

Each echoing hill, each verdant mount,
Their grateful praises who shall count;
What votive whispers stir the breeze,
Respondent from the bending trees !

Loud sounding praises forests fill,
The young bird warbles near the rill ;
The insect chirrups 'neath the sod ;
All, all, uplift the voice to God.

Earth's mighty magnates lowly bow,
Prostrate the nations bend the brow,
Joyous in praise the princes sing,
To Him, the Sovereign—Heaven's King.

Life's each extreme, the aged, the child,
Fervid in heart, in voice though mild,
With bashful maidens, vigorous youth,
Together chant His love, His truth.

Exalted He—to Him alone,
Obedience earth and heaven own ;
Obedience to His sacred name,
Aloud hear heaven and earth proclaim.

And ye ! at evening, noon and morn,
His best beloved—upraised your horn,
Ye saints who hear His hallow'd word,
Ye, Israel's children, bless the Lord !

———o———

THE DEATH OF EMILY BRONTÉ.

(PARAPHRASED FROM HER SISTER'S LETTER ON THAT SUBJECT.)

FREE from pain and sickness now,
In this world no more enduring;
Care no more shall shade her brow,
 Death, eternal peace securing;
Quenched her spirit's vigorous fire,
Bright—yet fleeting ere the morrow,
Short, but hard, her conflict dire,
Sorrow—sorrow—sorrow—sorrow !

E'en the day we hopeful thought,
Yet some weeks she still might tarry;
Soul its native heavens sought,
Could we—would we—death's dart parry ?
Quietly sad, her wasted frame,
We 'neath the hallowed pavement placed;
Breathing soft our sister's name,
Slowly home our steps retraced.
Very calm—our hearts resigned;
Who that saw her pain and anguish,
Would for longer life have pined,
In longer woe to see her languish ?
We know, we feel, she is at peace,
From piercing wind and bitter frost,
Haply freed she claims release,
Poor spirit, sadly "tempest toss'd."

Had she but lived—but why repine,
On thoughts like these we dare not dwell,
Her fate, my brother's, chance soon mine,
Again shall tone the church-yard knell.
Familiar faces—home endearing,
Fading—withering—vanished—gone—
Woe! woe to him, who trembling, fearing,
Sees them passing one by one.
But 't is God's will; be praised His grace ;
For good, of earthly cares bereft,
We know our last abiding place,
Is better far than that we left.

———o———

SACRED DREAMS.

A SCRIPTURE ENIGMA.

In visions of the darksome night,
Foretelling in His wondrous might,
Almighty power hath oft revealed,
What else had been from man concealed.

I.

To check the monarch's purposed scheme,
In warning came the threatening dream ;
When justified and free from blame,
Him guiltless doth the dream proclaim.

II.

An exile from his father's home,
A pious man was doomed to roam;
Though hard his couch, what dreams delight—
God! and his glorious angels bright!

III.

In after years when homeward bent,
Harsh foes would spoil his peaceful tent,
The Syrian's foul design is checked,
" The dream by night " doth still protect.

IV.

How innocent and artless seems
That loved one, who recounts his dreams,
Prophetic of his future state,
But woe for him whom brethren hate!

V.

Skilled to explain the mystic truth,
In prison see that injured youth
Interpret dreams, that one doth glad,
While hopeless one is trembling sad.

VI.

Mysterious where the corn and kine
Are heralds of the will divine,
The wise men stand amazed around;
The captive doth these dreams expound.

VII.

Boldly amid the adverse host,
The warrior takes his listening post;
From troubled visions hears the foe,
Predict their own sad overthrow.

VIII.

Assaying, God in slumber's dream,
What Israel's king would precious deem,
With glory graced that diadem
Where wisdom formed its brightest gem.

IX.

But not like him that monarch vain,
Furious would have the wise men slain,
But that, God-taught, the Hebrew youth
Revealed the awful vision's truth.

X.

So ye, although at first perplexed,
With God's aid seek the holy text,
Propound what here half-hidden seems,
Your senses wake to sacred dreams.

——o——

BREVITY OF LIFE.

ימי שנותינו בהם שבעים ישנה

תהלים צ "י

"The days of our years are threescore years and ten." Ps. xc. 10.

"THREESCORE and ten," the youth replies,
"How far off seems that day ;"
"Threescore and ten," the old man cries,
"How quickly pass'd away."

That lengthened life too short appears,
Which wronged nor injured any ;
If passed in sin, our youthful years,
Though few, are all too many.

WHERE TO PRAY.

בכל מקום אשר אזכיר את שמי אבא אליך וברכתיך
שמות כ' כד'

"In all places where I record my name,
I will come to thee and bless thee." Exodus xx. 24.

Is it on the mountain top,
　　We best can worship Thee?
Is it on the wide-spread plain,
　　Most reverent we should be?
Is it on the swelling deep,
　　We best can breathe the prayer;
Or is it in the flowery mead,
　　We should the hymn prepare?

Plaintive through the solemn woods,
　　The "still small voice" be heard?
'Mid the city's ceaseless toil,
　　His wondrous works revered?
Stately halls exultingly
　　Re-echo with Thy might;
Humble peasants eloquent,
　　Invoke Thy glorious light.

Need we tread the sacred fane,
　　There only, God to seek?
Temples wide the world outspreads,
　　In all, His praise to speak.
Ocean—earth—the wide extent,
　　Alike His house of prayer;
Where'er invoked, the God of love
　　Will come and bless us there.

"ICH DIEN."

AIR, "The Standard Bearer."

"At the battle of Crecy, the king of Bohemia, though then eighty
years old and entirely deprived of sight, insisted upon being led to
the field—he being at that time an ally of France. He fell, as might
have been expected, at the first encounter, and his crest, a plume of
ostrich feathers, being found after the conflict, was, with his motto
'Ich Dien,' adopted by Edward as the future heraldic distinction of
the Prince of Wales."

'MID Crecy's valiant field of fight,
　　There floats a snow-white pluméd crest,
It decks the helm of bravest knight,
　　That foremost e'er in battle pressed.
No youthful blood now fills his veins,
　　His once bright eyes are sightless seen,
But nought his gallant soul restrains,
　　Or checks his battle-cry " Ich Dien."

Though fourscore years had bowed his head,
　　Bohemia's king in faith was true,
When Edward's hosts o'er Gallia spread,
　　To aid his friends the veteran flew.
Allied to France—once more his heart,
　　Bade glitter forth his falchion keen,
Once more resumed the hero's part,
　　And once more sounds his cry, " Ich Dien."

He falls! his noble course is run ;
  The Black Prince brave, his valour heeds,
And when the field of Crecy's won,
  Thus honours he his valiant deeds :
"Be this pure crest of spotless white,
  Henceforth 'mid England's trophies seen,
By princes claimed—their proudest right,
  Their motto, guide, and faith, 'Ich Dien.'"

———o———

LA PREMIÈRE DANSEUSE.

(FROM AN UNPUBLISHED WORK OF THE AUTHOR'S.)

SOME years ago, my sister had frequent occasions to go
to the Docks, and in her perambulations in that not
very desirable locality, had more than once noticed a
young girl, whose wan and wretched appearance had
excited her commiseration, though there was not
sufficient distress apparent to make an offer of unso-
licited charity other than offensive. She was, as my
sister described her, of very graceful proportions, which
her slight vestments showed in their full contour. Of a
clear olive complexion, such as only Italia's skies could
ripen, though sunk with grief and care, her eyes yet
told how bright they must have been in happier hours.
Very thinly clad, though the weather was bleak in the
extreme ; she wore a slight gauze dress, apparently the
cast-off of some *élégante's* ball dress ; and thin silk shoes,
while they disclosed a graceful tapered ankle, were but
poor protection against the mud and snow, through
which she was compelled to pass.

My sister had often observed this young woman with kind inclination, and longed to address her; when, one evening, she again encountered the interesting stranger. Slowly and dispiritedly she seemed to walk, now leaning against the railing of a house, now looking as if to heaven for support, till, at length, exhausted nature gave way, and she sank at the feet of my sister, who was hastening to accost her. With the assistance of the bystanders she was raised, and her lodging having been pointed out, thither did Helen (my sister) accompany the senseless object of their care; but how shocked was her gentle soul at the sight that met her view. After ascending several flights of creaking and dirty stairs, a small attic was indicated as the young girl's chamber. With the exception of a miserable truckle-bed and two broken chairs it was literally empty, save that a large and massive ebony crucifix was appended in front of the chimney, as if religion was a support even in the depths of misfortune.

Depositing her on the wretched mattress, the old crone who owned the miserable hovel exclaimed, "Ah, poor creature, I thought how it would end, a penny loaf is but scanty living for two days. It was well she paid me that last shilling for lodging, or I don't know where she would have slept; poor creature, I am quite sorry for her, though she is a furrener." The unfeeling Sycorax was then leaving the room, but Helen hastily giving her money, bade her procure immediate relief and sustenance for the exhausted girl. This having been administered, slowly did she return to consciousness, and in the purest Tuscan offer her thanks to her benefactress, not considering that her language might not be understood. Answered unexpectedly in

F

her native dialect, an unrepressed emotion of mingled grief and pleasure took possession of her faculties, and falling on my sister's neck she wept aloud.

*   *   *   *

At a subsequent period, at Helen's request, she thus related her history—

"*O mia bella Patria!*   Dear loved Italy! shall I ever again behold thee? shall I ever again rove in thy myrtle bowers, or sport in thine orange groves? Thy vines are twined in purple clusters, never more for me to gather; and thy laurels still are fresh—but for me no more. And thou, too, loved lake, dream-revisited Como, with thy placid glass-like tide, reflecting tree and sky and mount, and thy gondolas swiftly gliding through the moonlit waves, and thy freshening air, and thine eternal brightness—but for me, all dim, all sad, all hopeless.

"I was born at Bellano, on the borders of the lake; my parents were poor, but honest and industrious, with rather a numerous family, of whom I was the youngest, and of course the favourite. Even from my childhood, I used to have for a companion the son of a neighbouring vintager; wherever I was, there was young Paulo by my side; we walked together, talked together, romped, laughed, and played together; in short, we were inseparable. Where was Paulo, you might be sure, my mother said, to find Nina; and if his father wished for his absent son, he had but to call my name, and we were both at his knee.

"So we grew, the village gossips already coupled us, and the old man smiled and patted my head, when I asked if I should not be his little daughter. One year glided thus after another, and I was the happiest

girl in all Italy. The days passed in healthful employment, and in the evenings we would dance under the
shade of the chestnut, and in the balmy fragrance of
the jasmine and the myrtle.

"Sometimes, too, Paulo would row me on the lucid
lake, and point out each well-known locality to my
view; and there we would trace the beauties dimpling
in smiles on nature's cheek, and like a rich carcanet
round an eastern satrap's neck, we would note the
bright emerald green of the olive and the cork trees,
and the sparkling ruby and the rich amethyst of the
grape, and the gold-enwrought groves of orange; while
studded here and there, like orient pearls, you might
see marble villas shining in whiteness beneath a sky of
sapphire, and tinted in the rich opaline hues of the
setting sun. Then the moonlight would come, and I
would cling closer to my companion, while he would
tell me tales of bandits and of robbers; and I would
look to the dim distance of the Alps, rising in the back
ground of this glorious amphitheatre, and fancy a
brigand in every bush and a musket in every fir tree.

"Two gentlemen had been in our neighbourhood for
a few days; they had hired a gondolet, but being unacquainted with its management, had, by inadvertance,
overset it in the very view of our cottage. Paulo immediately cut the rope of a fishing-boat from its moorings,
and with my father hastened to their assistance. With
difficulty they were saved, and were borne to our house,
where they received every attention. In the evening,
the elder gentleman, who was a merchant in Paris,
proposed, in the exuberance of his gratitude, to take
his young preserver, educate him, and receive him in
his counting-house. His father gladly availed himself

of this offer, which, on Paulo communicating to me,
with eyes brimful of tears, I would not be so selfish as
to wish him to decline.

"We had been dancing the Tarantella together, and
as our guests were looking at us, with a little excusable
vanity I was endeavouring my best; but I danced
no more that evening. As business required Mons.
Delmar to be in Paris, the morrow was fixed for their
departure. We had short time for leave-taking; Paulo
promised to learn to write the more quickly, that he
might write to me; and I recollect that, almost before
my eyes were dry, I took an old mass book, over which
I was toiling for some hours, in the hopes of being
enabled to read what he might learn to write.

"But it seemed as if fate willed that we should both
leave home at nearly the same time. The younger
gentleman, whom Paulo had saved, was manager of
La Scala, at Milan, and he offered my parents to train
me as a dancer for the opera. An affair of such moment was referred by my mother to the Confessor of the
village, and, as Father Geronimo assented, the proposal
was accepted by my parents. For myself, Paulo had
left, and since I could not be with him, I was careless
where I was.

"If I tell you how indifferent I was to all that surrounded me, on my transfer from our quiet village to
the bustling gaieties of the city, you may judge how
deeply my feelings were absorbed. It might have been
expected that, to a simple country girl like myself, all
would have been excitement and wonder. No! I was
listless and careless, there seemed no attraction in
novelty, no amusement in variety; I was sad at heart.
The Director, who I must say, treated me as kindly as

would a parent, used every endeavour to cheer me, and his daughters, grateful for their father's preservation, were almost as sisters to me. They would take me wherever they thought I might find enjoyment or amusement. Sometimes to the public walks or gardens, which were always well attended; and where we would see the gay, graceful, and glittering groups, gliding luxuriously under the cooling shades of the trees, or listening with enthusiasm to the military music, which enlivened the lustrous throng. Sometimes we would drive to the Corso, amid noble equipages and splendid equipments, and they would point out to my view the long line of Milanese nobility and Italian aristocracy that followed each other in quick succession, while the rich uniform of the Austrian hussar added to the gorgeousness of the scene. All this delighted me not; nor when all classes united in merriment at the attractive movements of Policinello could I join, in the joyous sounds.

"But I preferred going to the churches, which are in Milan both numerous and splendid, for I could kneel at the altars and pray for him there unchecked. Whether it was in the ancient aisles of the Basilica Ambrosiana or in any of the numerous churches of the Madonna, or mid the singular Gothic architecture of Il Duomo, thronged with its thousand statues and gemmed with its jewelled shrines, I passed with rapidity through the varied beauties of painting or sculpture to kneel at the foot of the altar, where I breathed prayers for his happiness in preference to my own.

"Certainly, one sight did succeed in exciting my attention, and I must, indeed, have been insensate not to have noticed it. The magnificent view that met my gaze on ascending to the spire of the Cathedral far exceeded the utmost limits of my imagination. The spire, which overtopping a mountain of the whitest marble, is itself an object of notice and admiration for miles around, is surrounded by a gallery, to which the spectator arrives by a flight of about 500 steps; but well and amply is the ascent repaid. Almost a shout burst from my lips at the gorgeous prospect; overcome with rapture I gasped for respiration. Immediately below me was the splendid city, with its beautiful irregularity of architecture, conspicuous among which was the noble square in which the Cathedral is situate. The eye, glancing over the city, encounters a well cultivated and highly fertile country, intersected in every direction with liquid mirrors, reflecting on their surface in multiplied continuity a bright unbroken line, which might seem another Eden. Vineyards, olive-yards, orchards, and orange groves were scattered in rich profusion, while extensive cultivations of rice, sloping to the water's-edge, waved in their verdant vegetation.

" Further away, like an extended plain below, lay Piedmont, Lombardy, with my own loved Como, and the Venetian States, which might well justify our claim as the garden of Europe; while innumerable towns and hamlets, studded with spire and turret, gave diversity, while they did not diminish the beauty of the scenery. Away in the far expanse of this glorious view was the snow-girt boundary of the Alps, with the pinnacle of Mont Blanc distinctly visible at the distance of 120 miles. To the south, the dark blue of the Apennines checked the gaze over Parma and Tuscany, which would seem to stretch to perpetuity.

" By the kind care of the director I was well educated, and at the Seminario I profited by instructions from first-rate artistes, and, after some time, was deemed competent for a *début* as principal dancer in the ballet. Nearly all this time I had been receiving letters which had been forwarded by Paulo to Bellano, and even while the writing was scarcely distinct to the eye, it was legible to the heart. But not having heard from him for three months, I was more than usually dull when the evening arrived for my first appearance. The director was in despair; great expectations had been raised respecting my performance, and I was angry with myself for my want of spirits, when one of the attendants delivered me a letter which had just arrived, and in an instant, like magic, its endearing words worked regeneration. The opera had concluded, and the curtain had risen for the ballet.

"Those who know how eagerly the appearance of a *debutante* is watched in Italy, will not be surprised at the numbers that had attended. It was a mythological ballet on the Judgment of Paris, in which I played the part of Venus. With palpitating heart I waited for the time of my entrance, resolved to strain every energy for success, for success pointed, through a long vista, to the completion of my hopes, a reunion with Paulo. Strange enough, except at rehearsals, I had never been at the theatre; and now, when it burst on me in its full splendour, I was absolutely dazzled and astounded.

"La Scala is reckoned the finest theatre in Europe, not even inferior to that of San Carlo at Naples; this magnificent building, brilliantly illuminated, and blazing in the richness of wealth and beauty, was thronged to the roof. The scenery and decorations were worthy its noble tenantry, while the orchestra, at all times in

Italy an object of national interest, more particularly so at Milan, was numerous and select. The first sensation of astonishment and wonder having subsided, I entered into the duties of my character, at first with great timidity, but, acquiring fresh courage and resolution from the possession of my lately received letter, and the associations it inspired, I astonished myself, and, while applauding testimonials stamped the seal of approval, even my kind friend, the director. Suffice it, I was eminently successful, and at once attained the summit of my profession. Liberally repaid for my exertions, I was enabled to render my parents many comforts, nor was I slow to acquaint my youthful companion of my good fortune; about this time, however, his patron had removed his establishment from Paris, and my letters did not reach him.

"After a bright career at Milan, I was successively engaged at Venice, Naples, Florence, Rome, and all the principal cities of Italy; and I, who but a few years back, had been rambling unheeded on the banks of my native lake, was now as the "brilliant Dellcomo," receiving admiration, protestations, valuable presents, and flattering praise from the mighty and the noble. Most eagerly was my presence sought, and most lavish offers of engagement were made to secure my services. At one time I had offers lying on my boudoir from Vienna, Berlin, Paris, London, and even from St. Petersburg, without reckoning others from various parts of Italy and Germany. My decision was soon formed; it was for Paris, though certainly the proposal from that capital was not the most lucrative. Received with all the honours and attention that might await a noble guest, flattered and fêted, I felt more desire to seek the residence of Mons. Delmar, than to avail myself of the enjoyments offered for my participation.

"My professional engagements, and those civilities, which, without rudeness, I could not entirely decline, considerably occupied my attention, so that it was at the close of my Parisian engagement that I learned the removal of the worthy merchant to Lyons, much crippled in his resources. Thither then was my next stage, in spite of eager and very tempting offers to prolong my stay at Paris. My journey was of no avail, M. Delmar, heart-stricken at his misfortunes, and sinking under their rapid accumulation, had been attacked with paralysis, which eventually was the cause of his death. The business was broken up, and the employés had gone, no one knew whither. Letters to Bellano were also fruitless, Paulo had not been heard of there. Even amid all the luxury in which I had been moving, I still looked back with fond retrospection to those happy hours of youth, and I could not but regret the loss of one, whom every succeeding year had but the more endeared to me.

"It has too long been the idea, that vice and debauchery are inseparable companions from the mode of existence which I followed. To a certain extent it may be true, that females, exposed to a theatrical life, acquire a taint from the moral atmosphere which they breathe. But not from innate vice do they swerve; if they fall, it is not from want of principle, but from circumstances which they are powerless to control. Cajoled and caressed by those whose sole object is to deceive; scarcely heeded by those of their own sex whose protection might shield, and whose counsels might guide; treading 'mid the mazy paths of luxury and excitement — can we wonder, that lured by false lights, they may stray from the right ways, and become entangled in the labyrinth. Walking amid burning ploughshares, it is well for those who come unscathed from the ordeal. From my own knowledge can I speak of those tempting baits that shine but to decoy, of the fine woven nets spread but to ensnare.

"In many of the continental cities have I been exposed to those shameless proposals, which men, otherwise of the best sentiments, think it no shame to offer to a female, whose career may be, as mine was, on the stage. I take little praise for saying, I repulsed with indignation these insults. But it was in England, moral as I had always thought it, that I was exposed to the most continuous repetition of this degradation; and with a perseverance worthy a better cause was I persecuted. Often after enrapturing brilliant crowds at the Opera house, have I retired to my bed, to weep at the insolence of some profligate lordling, or decrepid debauchee, who pursued me with licentious obsequiousness. My obstinacy, so my resolution was termed, was deemed a fault; and I, who but the season before was termed a second Terpsichore, now was almost deserted. New divinities appeared, more propitious they said, and a determined and ungenerous opposition was in progress against me. Forgive me that I ascribe these unworthy motives to your countrymen, but, in fact, so determined a party was raised against me, that the manager, in self-defence, was compelled to rescind my engagement.

"Indignant at this illiberal treatment, I hastened home to prepare for immediate departure for the Continent; when judge my consternation at beholding my chamber in a state of disorder, the drawers stripped of their valuable contents, and my escritoire, which had contained a large amount in money and jewels, completely

rifled. The agitation which I suffered by this sudden
deprivation threw me into a fever, from which it was
many months before I recovered. During this illness,
I exhausted nearly my whole remaining resources, and
found myself, on my protracted convalescence, in a
strange land, without friends, without money, without
resources. Hope of return to my former employment
was fruitless; it was with difficulty I could even walk;
and I, who had been the idolised of many, now was
deserted by all. I removed to more humble apartments,
and contrived by the sale of my remaining necessaries,
to eke out a wretched life. I sought some whom I had
assisted in my prosperity, but I was the "stricken
deer," and they bade me "go weep." Could I have
reached Italy, there I had yet a home, but that was
denied me. So day by day I sank in wretchedness,
never, believe me, in wrong, though persecuted with its
tempters; at length, with exhausted purse, I sought
this wretched hovel, where I have laboured, with what
skill I might, to drag on a wearisome existence, till
weakened nature denied her aid. Need I tell you all is
gone; all, save that crucifix at whose feet, with Paulo,
I oft have knelt; it has been my constant companion,
my never failing supporter, my mother's gift from
Como. *O mia bella Patria!* "

* * * * *

It would be too long to tell, how restored to health,
Nina was enabled again to repair to her own land, and
to occupy a farm and vineyard, which, with happy fore-
thought she had purchased in the days of her prosperity,
and where, by a fortunate chain of circumstances, she
was united for life to the loved companion of her
youth, her never-forgotten Paulo.

APOLOGY FOR LOVING.

BLAME me not for loving thee ;
　　Could I e'er discover,
The glimpse of but a fault in thee,
　　I'd be no more a lover.

But while I trace, fair maid, in thee,
　　The presence of each charm,
How can I from such graces flee,
　　My passion to disarm ?

Then blame me not, that still I love,
　　I know, alas ! 'tis vain
To raise my thoughts so high above,
　　Yet can I not refrain.

——o——

THE STOLEN HEART.

(IMITATED FROM HERRICK.)

SAY, was it kindly done of thee,
　　To steal away my heart,
And when I would have one for me,
　　Refuse with thine to part ?

It is not fair, thus to retain,
   A stolen heart like mine;
Yet would I, dearest, not complain,
   To barter, love, for thine.

If still you act the miser's part,
   To covet all you can,
And still you prize that pilfered heart,
   Take with the heart—the man.

—o—

"EN ATTENDANT."

As watching long at heaven's gate,
With faith new-sprung and hope elate,
Awhile expectant spirits wait,
   Admission there:
And all the day-beams of the thought,
That heaven long and earnest sought,
By penitence is early bought,
   And faith and prayer.

So I, who wait so anxiously,
Thy beaming smile again to see,
Yet while the minutes seem to be,
   Each one an hour,
I blame not then the sad delay,
Anticipation paves the way,
And light, the harbinger of day,
   Pervades thy bower.

Long in the sea the diver lies,
But now he bears to wondering eyes,
From ocean cave, the treasured prize,
   His toil repays.
So, as the time-tide hastens o'er,
I miss thy presence more and more,
But ah! again the brightened shore—
   I meet thy gaze.

—o—

EMIGRATION.

(A COMIC EFFUSION.)

SINCE now-a-days there's many a man
   Attempting Emigration,
Why should not I propose a plan
   To benefit the nation;
Long have I thought in my mind
   To find a fitting home,
Might seem by Nature's self designed
   For kindred souls to roam.

The brewers should to Malta go,
   The loggerheads to Scilly,
The quakers to the Friendly Isles,
   And the furriers all to Chili.
The little bawling squalling elves,
   Who break our nightly rest,
While their nurses haste to Babylon,
   Go to Lapland or to Brest.

From Spithead, cooks run over Greece,
    And while the miser waits
His passage to the Guinea Coast,
    The spendthrift's in the Straits.
To Geneva quick will drunkards hie,
    At the Needles spinsters be,
While gourmands lunch at Sandwich Isles,
    'Twill suit them to a T.

Musicians hasten to the Sound,
    The surplus priests to Rome,
While all the race of hypocrites
    At Canton are at home;
Send Bachelors to the United States,
    Maids to the Isle of Man,
Let gardeners all to Botany go,
    And shoeblacks to Japan.

While debtors flock to Ohio,
    And poets to the Meuse,
The firemen to the Indians go,
    And to Greenland all the blues.
Most lovers rest pleased with Good Hope,
    To some the Horn gives pain,
The cockneys pause to Lyons see,
    Bold sailors cross the Maine.

The stationer, post, inquires for Rheims,*
    Blacklegs for Wight design,
While rogues may find a longitude
    That's just below the Line.

---

* All proper names to be read as an Englishman would pronounce
them, *e.g.*, Reams.

Run surgeons to Connecticut,
　　Finland's the Sharks' abodes,
While half our idle vagabonds
　　Might mend their ways in Rhodes.

———o———

RED RIDING HOOD

(SET TO MUSIC BY MR. P. VAN NOORDEN).

IN a neatly built cottage just down by the wood,
There lived with her mother, little Red Riding Hood ;
To a neighbouring village one morning she went,
With kindest of wishes to Grandmamma sent,
With a pot of fresh butter, and a half-pound of tea,
The one was choice Dorset, the other Bohea.
" Now hasten, my darling," her mother did say,
" And stop not to gossip or sport on the way."

She was leaving the wood, when a wolf she espied ;
" Good morning, Miss Riding Hood," the animal cried,
" Pray where are you walking this morning so fine ? "
" To see my dear gran'ma my course I design ;
A pot of fresh butter, and tea, too, I take,
And see here, mamma has sent a nice cake."
Says the wolf, " I'll be first there, let's run then a race."
Away then he scampered at swiftest of pace.

He soon reached the cottage, found the grandma in bed,
Ate up the old dame, put her cap on his head,
Then jumped in her place, scarce got there before
He heard a loud tapping outside the cot door.

"Come in, my sweet darling," the hypocrite cried,
"There put down your basket, and sit by my side;
Now read me a book my time to amuse;
Pray how is your mother, and what is the news?"

"Dear gran'ma," she said, as she looked with surprise,
"How harsh is your voice, and how large are your eyes!"
"The better to see with." "And then your big nose!"
"The better to smell with, you'll own, I suppose."
"What great ears you've got, and then what big teeth!"
"The better to eat with." So he sprang from beneath
The blankets and sheets upon poor Riding Hood,
And gobbled her up like the daintiest food.

And now I am thinking, if 'stead of delaying
To talk to the wolf she had not been staying,
But heeded her mother, and quickly walked on,
The wolf had not known where 't was she had gone;
The granny had lived to drink tea and eat cake,
Her little granddaughter with her would partake.
Let children all then be obedient and good,
And be warned by the fate of poor Red Riding Hood.

————o————

BLUE BEARD,

A COMIC VERSION.

(SET TO MUSIC BY MR. P. E. VAN NOORDEN.)

ONE day said Blue Beard to his spouse,
"I'm off to town this morning;
Here, take the keys of all the house,
But listen to my warning;

G

In every room you wish to go,
　　My leave you have to enter,
Except the one that's just below,
　　The blue room in the centre.   (*Repeat.*)

This is the key; now pray attend;
　　Look well, its bright and *chub*-by."
Says she, "You may on me depend;
　　Good-bye, my darling hubby."
But scarcely gone, his words she mocks,
　　In every room doth venture,
At length she turns the little locks
　　Of the blue room in the centre.

She screamed, she squalled, she saw a sight,
　　For wives lay round about, dead,
Like porter that has stood all night,
　　Each wife was flat—without head!
The key she dropped, it turned all rust,
　　In vain was all her rubbing;
"Bless me," says she, " here'll be a dust,
　　Oh! sha'nt I catch a drubbing."

Blue Beard came home, she gave the keys,
　　Says he, "I think I miss one."
"Here 't is."   "Ha! ha! pray, if you please,
　　How came the stain on this one?
One hour I give, go say your prayers,
　　You would not heed my warning,
Be off—despatch—come quick downstairs,
　　For you must die this morning."

From out the tower looked sister Anne,
   To see if help was near them,
No help was there of boy or man,
   Nor brothers' aid to cheer them.
" Come down !" said Blue Beard, with a roar,
   " Your faults shall now be paid of,"
But the brothers rushed in through the door,
   And shaved his beard and head off.

—o—

APPLES OF GOLD IN FRAMES OF SILVER.

PROVERBS XXV. 11.

(INSCRIBED TO MR. M. MONTAGU ON THE COMPLETION OF HIS
VERSION OF THE PSALMS;

COMPARED WITH THE HEBREW, ANNOTATED AND REVISED
BY THE AUTHOR OF "AUTUMN GATHERINGS.")

WHEN erst inspired the royal Psalmist wrote
The matchless hymns which countless myriads quote,
When erst in words outspoke his raptured mind,
Poetic grace with pious thoughts combined
To raise, to cheer, to sanctify mankind.

When, sad his voice, he told his anguished plaint,
How foes pursued, his soul who would attaint ;
How wicked men who sought his life to snare,
Though guiltless he, would not their rage forbear ;
Sunk in distress he wails his cares, his woes :
Yet see ! 'mid gloom what cheering hope-fire glows,
'Mid darkness see ! a glorious light illumes !
His trust, ne'er failing, all its strength resumes ;
Refuge is nigh, and mark that evil band,
Now quivering sink, beneath his God's right hand.

Deliverance-songs now Israel's bards up take,
Deliverance-songs the choral band awake,
To God on high up-peals th' harmonious hymn,
To God enthroned amid the cherubim ;
'Mid Salem's shrines and Zion's echoing mounts,
New songs of gladness now each voice recounts,
And chiefly there amid the exulting throng,
Hear Israel's king loud chant the grateful song.

When holy days and times of sacred note,
Saw gathering crowds from distant lands remote,
Far off was heard, like sound of flower-fed bees,
A hum as soft as zephyr's gentle breeze ;
It fills the air, now louder swells the voice,
Exulting bids the heaven and earth rejoice ;
It nearer comes with myrtle wreath and palm,
The festal welcome—blessed—the holy Psalm ;
From thousand voices hear the answering quire,
A thousand hands now strike the harp, the lyre ;
The heart with fervour bows in faith avowed,
Rejoicing hymns now thrill that gladsome crowd :
Happy those days—their own lov'd land they trod,
They sang their sacred ode and praised their God.

When sickness came with strength-prostrating power,
When sad distress o'erclouded life's bright hour,
When fading friends and failing health combined,
And Jesse's son seemed shunned of all mankind,
By man forsaken, aid of God he sought ;
Here in these Psalms bright inspiration fraught.
Here in these Psalms we learn how God e'er deigns
To raise the fallen—how His power sustains

The humble pious—the orphan to secure,
In hope He bids the widow's faith endure ;
From death's own grasp, from 'neath the oppressor's rod,
Here see displayed the might of mercy's God ;
Relieved from woe, from want, from dire distress,
Then would the soul its votive thanks express,
The grateful thanks with which the mind o'erteems,
Seek in these Psalms for gratitude's best themes.

But not for them alone these gems designed,
For Israel's race—ah ! no—for all mankind ;
Not doom'd like fleeting verse to gild an hour,
These words of worth—this mighty valued dower ;
Not for one age—for centuries—all time,
Not for one soil—for all—for every clime ;
Where'er o'er earth the steps of man had ranged,
His faithful guide, his comforter unchanged ;
While earth endures exhaustless treasures yield,
This richest mine, this ever fertile field.

But vain their hope long time to share who sought,
The treasured gems—the store of hallowed thought ;
Unskilled—for them, alas ! in sacred lore,
In vain they sought to share the priceless store ;
With anxious eyes the Hebrew child they saw
From this loved book his holiest rapture draw ;
In vain attempts to reach the light they fail,
Their powerless efforts cannot pierce the veil.

Now see, with patient toil some pious hand,
Essays the task, and lo ! each grateful land,
In its own tongue now reads these words of worth,
These words of heaven kindly lent to earth ;

And now so blessed how joyed the nations band ;
What rapturous hymns resound throughout each land ;
To all, to each, some blessing and some balm,
The holy fanes now peal with each loved Psalm ;
Again essayed the men of pious heart,
Each tried his skill and taxed poetic art ;
From his own store some new-born grace bade spring,
Some charm of thought, some new-turn'd rhyme to bring,
To roundelays or strains of amorous note,
Erewhile their skill who did of yore devote :
How changed their themes—the Gallic poet sings,[1]
And hallowed verse pervades the court of kings ![2]

Here in this land—here too—long past the time,
Holy the thought yet feeble in the rhyme,
When savage Henry ruled with vengeful power,
And made religion plaything of an hour,
Then men[3] too powerless for the task they sought,
('T was strange the task no inspiration brought),
To halting verse for public service meant,
Transposed these odes of music eloquent,—
Would that their skill had equalled their intent.

Though scant its worth, long time this version seemed
Meet for church use, for sacred service deemed,
Till now 't was thought in second Charles—his time,
Quaint in its phrases, faulty in its rhyme ;
And lo ! there sprang another twin-born text,[4]
Where oft confused the mind is sorely vexed
To trace the import of the sense perplexed ;

. [1] Clement Marot.   [2] Francis the First, etc.
[3] Sternhold and Hopkins.   [4] Tate and Brady.

Yet stamp'd with fiat of the state command,
Fearless of rivals firm these medleys stand,
And rule unquestioned e'er throughout the land.

Bright reason now demands a chaster muse,
Poetic grace should o'er these hymns diffuse,
That, pleased the ear should to their beauties bend,
While holy words with sounds melodious blend;
And yet not dazzled by poetic beams,
Be still preserved the spirit of these themes;
Be still preserved the ancient Hebrew fire,
That warmed the bard—that woke the sacred lyre,
And tho' transfused these words "more pure than gold,"
Still must their sense, so loved in days of old,
Breathe in its pureness, in each hallowed verse,
Which pious hearts would to their God rehearse.

But where the man the task would boldly dare?
The wrongs of ages who would fain repair?
What various skill should in that man combine,
Would nobly venture on this proud design?
A heart replete with pious store of thought,
A mind serene with various knowledge fraught;
Wit to discern where oft the sense perplexed,
Sees light but glimmering in the mystic text;
A soul poetic, yet with care repressed,
Lest fancy-led but half the sense expressed,
In feeble imagery he attires the rest;
Or, lest extending to a needless length,
The text enfeebled loses all its strength.
Where seek the man of sense and faith combined,
Of pious fervour, wit, poetic mind,

Would free, release from old enfettering rules,
Would burst the bonds of Charles', of Henry's schools,
Would make these ways where now all toilsome plod,
Religion's road—a pleasant path to God!

Thine, Montagu! the noble task to dare,
The " pleasant path " anew to bid prepare,
To pluck the weeds that cumbering chock the way,
And crush the flowers thy care now bids display ;
The heart, the mind, the soul, that should combine,
In such a task, all, Montagu, are thine.
In fitting garb who David's Psalms now see,
With thankful heart will grateful think of thee ;
O, be they blessed, thy labours and thy care,
Long sound thy verses in the house of prayer ;
When pealing forth be these orisons given,
May each for thee some favour win from heaven ;
Through all the land may now thy verse rebound,
Responsive now let heart and voice resound ;
O, may thy words to good each heart incline,
And in their souls be—best reflected—thine ;
On earth their joy—in heaven their blessing, this
Like theirs, thy joy—like thine, their endless bliss !

——o——

ELEGY

ON THE DEATH OF BARONESS N. M. DE ROTHSCHILD.

(TRANSLATED FROM THE HEBREW OF H. E.)

THE stars are dimmed ; the sun withdraws each ray ;
    From every eye the streaming tears pour forth ;
Called to her sires ! alas ! how sad the day,
    When earth enfolds this form of glorious worth !

Grief and despair throughout the land abound,
  Men mourn their princess lost to mortal eyes,
While God's bright angels cheer with welcome sound,
  The advent of their sister to the skies.

Near to the helpless—she of noblest mind;
  Pride in her heart ne'er found a resting spot;
Not for display her liberal gifts designed,
  Secret in good, she cheered afflictions lot.
As bounteous rain, dispensed her generous store,
  With kindly grace she bids the poor one live;
Blessed with her gifts, the needy's woes are o'er,
  More wearied they to take than she to give.

Sadly for her the ranks of Judah mourn;
  The lorn one weeps her benefactress dead;
Each noblest heart, alike with anguish torn,
  The glorious crown is rent from off their head.

Angels of grace! from yon celestial heights,
  Look down, behold our tears, our grief-full hearts;
On every side one sad lament incites,
  When meek benevolence like hers departs.
Angels of grace! your sister's form sustain;
  Your sister she, while yet she lived on earth,
A mortal garb did then her limbs constrain,
  But now, like you, in all of heavenly worth.
O! valued soul! in kindred heaven dwell;
  There, where the saints in seven-fold gladness live;
Thy memory cherish those who loved thee well—
  Eternal bliss thy best reward will give.

———o———

ELEGY

ON THE DEATH OF BARONESS N. M. DE ROTHSCHILD.

(TRANSLATED FROM THE HEBREW OF B. H. A.)

DAUGHTER of Israel! thy sackcloth gird—strip off each
    garb of joy,
A mournful day o'er thee hath dawned—in grief your
    hours employ;
Weep! weep! for her; her children's hope—illustrious
    in her birth,
Our nation's pride; alas! hath fled this soul of noblest
    worth.

How vain *their* trust—how slight *their* prop, how fragile
    is their stay,
Support who seek, in treasured store, or empty gold's
    display!
Why boast the proud in idle vaunt? to wealth why
    homage yield?
When bursts o'er them the day of wrath, can then *their*
    idol shield?

Estranged from good, from virtue far—why lift the
    haughty head?
Gives then, thy gold, superior power—thou, and the
    poor one dead,
Alike ye lie, in kindred dust—low on your earthen
    floor—
How poor, then oft, the rich man's lot—how rich the
    needy's store!

O ! what is man—this powerless worm—this evanescent
    flower—
That simple he should sigh or grieve—more simply
    sport his hour !
A fleeting shadow mortal life—e'en to the grave from
    birth—
Then why thy care pangs, shadow, say ? or whence thy
    hollow mirth ?

The monarch's throne—how scant in worth, or pomp,
    or pride of state,
Arraigned, when stand for justice-doom, the lowly and
    the great !
What boots his empty span of years—his fruitless hopes
    or care,
If righteous deeds and virtuous life no monument
    prepare !

Exulting, those in God who trust, how joyful is their
    lot ;
Confiding—e'en at death's fell gates, they blanch, they
    tremble not ;
For them no gloom—'mid darkness, light, a glorious
    sparkling beam,
Aye ! e'en amid death's shadow shines, their virtue's
    radiant gleam.

Thou righteous woman ! happy thou ! blessed with all
    store of good,
How oft thine aid hath bid dispense bright learning's
    choicest food,

With fostering hand the poor didst raise! treasured in
    realms above,
Go seek thy meed—whose life on earth was charity and
    love.

Hear the lament! the widow's plaint, the orphan's
    saddened wail,
Bitter her sighs—thy anxious care—the mother in
    travail;
Who now relieve—who cheer our hearts—who give our
    sorrows ease,
Our fainting forms who now support—who clothe the
    limbs that freeze?

Steadfast in faith, such their career, and heavenly their
    reward,
Whose deeds secure eternal bliss, win favour from the
    Lord;
May life's best charms be those who mourn, from thee
    this truth who learn,
In God's own path of virtuous deeds, like thee, their
    course discern.

—o—

TRUST IN GOD.

לך ה״ קוינו לך ה״ ניחל

" In thee, O God! we hope; in thee, O God! we trust."

(Written in 1854.)

I.

DARK shades cloud o'er the earth, with mournfulness
    imbued,
Pensive, with downcast eyes, the sterile ground we
    viewed,

Wearied with vain regrets, we trod th' ungenial fields,
Its golden store the vacant barn now no longer yields.
Anxiously, with throbbing heart, tho stalwart workmen
    muse,
The bitter grief of mothers sad the hungry child
    bedews.
Nations trembling, shrink in awe, fearful rulers quail,
Mortal skill, a fragile reed, to check the foe's assail;
Downward, as with vulture-swoop, dart birds of omen
    dread,
So stalks grim-visaged famine, with deathlike fatal
    tread.
In vain were man's control—but thou, O Lord! art
    just,
In Thee, O God! we hope, in Thee alone we trust.

II.

Harsh as in forest wilds, outpeals the tiger's roar,
Reverberates a sound through Europe's every shore;
Brazen and rash defiance dares th' imperious North,
Sweet gentle peace affrightening, swells that wild cry
    forth;
Aroused, uprise the brave, the glittering falchions grasp,
Love-locked in last embrace, despairing maidens clasp;
Alas! alas! ere stills again that trumpet's bated breath,
Eyes brightly gleaming now will sleep in fearful death;
Thousands be of hope bereft, from home and homestead
    torn,
Ensanguined cities flame, and myriad hearts will
    mourn;
Yet will we bravely strive to stem that bad man's
    lust;
In Thee, O God! we hope; in Thee alone we trust.

III.

Pestiferous in the air hangs a fearful doom,
Corrupting light and life with odours of the tomb,
Crushing plants of hopeful bud, stems of goodly pride,
Pressing down the aged sire—the newly-wedded bride;
Poisoning with carrion breath the roseate darling's kiss,
Germinating ill from joy, and misery from bliss.
Ghastly figures fill our homes of anxiousness and dread;
They, who would the dear ones mourn, themselves are
    with the dead;
Famine and war and pestilence cloud the fated land,
Calamity threefold, can mortal man withstand;
Humanity is bowed, low to its kindred dust;
In Thee, O Lord! we hope; in Thee alone we trust.

IV.

Then to Thine indulgent ear prayers did we address,
Hearing from Thine holy hill assuaged was our distress;
Thou gav'st the word, and vanishing, night gave way
    to day,
Firm support in Thee we found, comfort, hope, and stay.
Famine hastes abashed to hide; amid the waving sheaves,
Pregnant with the teeming crop, earth's ample bosom
    heaves;
Shouts triumphant victory gladly from afar,
Heralding tranquillity, and stilling cruel war;
Thy balm of grace, medicinal, purifies the air,
Winning heartfelt gratitude to Thee "who hearest
    prayer,"
For Thy soft breath of mercy calms the tempest gust.
In Thee, O Lord! we hope; in Thee, O God! we trust.

HUMAN LIFE.

"The birds are the messengers of the Gods."

EURIPIDES.

IN my chamber musing, as I sat perusing
A book I oft am using, 't is Rogers' " Human Life ;"
Half calmness, half dejection, my thoughts without
    connection
In dreamy recollection of bygone peace and strife,
From out the fire-flame blazing, as listless I sat gazing,
I saw—O ! sight amazing ! a banner self-upraising,
       Its legend, Human Life.

My dreamy thoughts suspending, just then there came
    descending,
With early sun rays blending, a milk-white new-fledged
    Dove ;
The little fearless creature, so innocent in feature,
Seemed pupil both and teacher of faith and hope and
    love ;
In sportive happy winging, around my chamber flinging
Bright seeds, which, quick upspringing, bore flower
    buds, life-like singing,
       Of new-born Infant Life.

The roseate tints of morning, each tracery adorning,
Soon with sudden warning the silver wings unfold ;
And swift as it departed, down heaven's blue vault
    darted,

So swiftly that I started (while thrilling cadence rolled),
A blithesome Lark came flying, all practised skill out-
    vying,
With open throat defying, in rampant mirth outcrying,
        Like joyous Youthful Life.

Still rapt in fancy's tracing, sweetly interlacing,
I saw in soft embracing, two Love-birds fondly twined ;
The sun was in meridian, when (bold as warlike Gideon
Pursued the hosts of Midian, 'mid raging storm and
    wind),
Eye-balls crimson flushing, an Eagle fierce came rushing,
Those tender Love-birds crushing, from strife whose
    blood outgushing,
        Well symbolled Manhood's Life.

Ah me! "Love lies a-bleeding," the Eagle fierce
    unheeding,
Triumphantly was feeding on those two twins of light ;
Again the sun-blaze gleaming was in my chamber
    streaming,
And through its hottest beaming, shrieking the bird
    took flight.
Then twilight hour was shading, an ancient Owl came
    wading,
My solemn thoughts as aiding, like wisdom's tones
    pervading,
        O'er man's Declining Life.

Clouds of darkness rolling, saddened past controlling,
The distant knell was tolling, of parting human life ;
Sudden, without motion, my room seemed changed to
    ocean,

'Mid strains of pure devotion, resignation rife,
Its melody retaining, a dying Swan sustaining,
Life gone, but faith remaining, eternity thus gaining—
    Immortal Human Life !

——o——

EARLY CLOSING.

(AN EPIGRAM.)

" How's this ?" says one, " our neighbour Jew,
    At Saturday noon now closes ;
Methinks he must have read anew
    His boasted laws of Moses."

" The laws of Moses—no ! my friend,
    Think not he heeds such trifles,
His shop he shuts—because—attend—
    His shopmen joined the Rifles."

——o——

RESOLUTION AND AMENDMENT.

(ON A RECENT NOTICE BY A CO-RELIGIONIST.)

In consequence of resolutions passed,
    At Willis's Rooms proposed,
This shop will now from Sabbath last
    At two o'clock be closed.

H

AMENDMENT.

In consequence of resolutions passed,
   At Sinai's mount proposed,
While holy Sabbath day doth last
   This shop is ever closed.

—o—

THE CHOICE.

If it were left for me to choose,
   Or heaven alone or earth with thee,
Elysium's hopes I would refuse,
   Content on earth to roam with thee;
For what were heaven's joys to me,
   Or what the bliss I there might know,
Unshared, those joys could only be
   An endless, lengthened dream of woe.

Though angel eyes might greet me there,
   In all their bright cerulean hue,
Yet e'en their smiles could not compare
   With that fond glance in thee I view.
Though cherub lips might speak my praise,
   And seraph eyes might watch my rest,
O! where's the heart mid heaven's rays,

   Like that which beats within thy breast.
This dream of life will soon be o'er,
   Our souls will then be free to roam,
And when they reach the mystic shore,
   Each then will seek its destined home;

But if by fate I'm doom'd to rise,
  And leave thee pining there below,
My soul will spurn those cloudless skies,
  And blest with thee, e'en heaven forego.

———o———

FOREST GLINTON.

A CHARACTER, FROM LIFE.

IN these days of railroads and steamboats, so trivial an
incident as a passage to the Continent is scarcely worth
mentioning; it was not so half a century back, the
delay, the *désagrémens* and the thousand accidents which
which were sure to beset the traveller, were almost
certain to involve adventures, more or less important in
their consequences. Acquaintances were sometimes
commenced, induced by trifling civilities, which at
other times would have been unheeded, and there were
not wanting many of the sharper-witted portion of the
community to take advantage of the unguarded con-
fidence too often displayed by the unthinking in the
course of a long journey. Particularly exposed to the
approaches of these disinterested friends were the
honest and confiding Englishmen, who, taking advantage of the recent peace, were flocking to France to
partake in the revelries of its gay metropolis.

When that universal leveller, sea-sickness, would
give me leisure to make my observations, I could not

but notice, with some degree of curiosity, the gradual approaches of one of these *remorae* of society into the good graces of as genuine an English family as ever left the fat fields of Suffolk to pay for peeping at foreign novelty As they were bound to Paris, I promised myself some amusement in watching their progress, at the same time with a chivalric intent to prevent their recently attached friend from taking too lively an interest in their welfare. This, I confess, was no business of mine, but there was such an honest simple-heartedness about the whole of this family, and having some previous knowledge of the character of their extempore acquaintance, I determined, if possible, to put them on their guard.

While I was engaged in forming schemes, for the interruption of manœuvres of which I supposed the Squire and his family to be the intended victims, I was unconscious of the endeavours of one of our fellow voyagers to ingratiate himself into my esteem. Indeed, so unobtrusive and so very gentlemanly were his approaches, such an air of refined breeding, and so inexhaustible a fund of information were at his command, that it was impossible not to be attracted by his demeanour; a friend who accompanied me, was equally captivated by the society of our intelligent companion.

Forest Glinton was a younger branch of a noble but comparatively necessitous family. Early in life he had been sent to one of our leading public seminaries, and subsequently to college, at both of which places he had distinguished himself by acquiring the highest academical distinctions. Yet his knowledge seemed to have come to him almost by intuition ; few could remember ever to have seen him studying,—there was not a horse race or a boating match, a private debauch or a public "town and gown contest," but Glinton was one of the *mêlée*. Yet, in all points of university lore, the syllogisms or sophisms of logic, the most obscure readings of the classics, or the most abstruse points of mathematics, he was never at fault. How this information was acquired was to many a mystery; many a freshman who watched his career, and had prepared to see him "plucked," wondered with staring eyes at the encomiums of the learned examiners, and resolved to try, if by a reckless course, like that of Forest Glinton, they might not be equally fortunate, and imbibe at once draughts from "the Piërian spring" with those from the fount of the Bacchic god. Simple youths! did they indeed fancy that this store of knowledge came to him by inspiration, or that Minerva, although in academic groves, would "unsought be won."

Little did they know that this indifference to study, like his every other act, was but simulated, was but part of what was his whole life, a living lie. Hours after hours, when the wearied companions of his midnight orgies would seek a fevered and an unquiet couch, in his little study, apart from the world's gaze, would he labour to acquire that information which was to astonish his fellow collegians on the morrow. Of a frame and constitution apparently soft and delicate as a girl's, but truly iron as his own heart, he could endure riotous revelries and excesses which would exhaust many of his robust companions. Seemingly as fatigued and as besotted as themselves, he would stagger to his chambers, where, divesting himself at once of his assumed intemperance, "like the lion shaking the dew

drops from his mane," he would, with all the energy of
his highly gifted mind, grapple with learned difficulties,
and overcome, as with a giant's strength, obstacles that
had mastered minds matured in wisdom.

Truly it was a paradox, yet is it not so oft in nature
—do we not see qualities the most opposite and uncongenial combine in one individual.   How beautiful the
soft glossiness and rich hues of the tiger's coat, yet
with what savage rapacity are these united!   What
soul-entrancing music thrills from beneath the dull
russet of the heaven-soaring lark,—what harsh ear-
grating sounds issue from the gorgeous throat of the
peacock!   Nature is no partial mother.   If to one of
her children she seem to bestow one gift in perfection,
be sure she has withheld from that favoured child some
other boon, the rightful heritage of his brother.   It is
thus when we lament the absence of a charm, the only
" unfinished window in the living palace," we are never-
theless forced to confess that our bounteous mother has
been just as she is generous, while so lavishly, yet so
considerately, dispensing her treasures.   Truly it is a
paradox ; yet how often do we see the qualities of the
body predominant, while those of the mind, which
would be such fitting attendants, alas! are sought for
in vain.   Or, if by a happy combination, these should
meet in one fortunate individual, where is the heart—
the bright sun that should illumine, that should irra-
diate, that should warm to life and healthful glow the
aspirations of the cultivated mind.

These reflections will not be misplaced, since they
will apply to our consideration of the characteristics
of Forest Glinton.

Of form and figure, as I have already mentioned,

femininely, yet not effeminately delicate, beautiful almost as a beautiful woman, and with a vigour of perception that could seize, as with the quickness of thought each passing incident, to mould or fashion at his will; with an energy of spirit that could pierce through the obscurity of time, and walk in proud communion with the olden men of renown,—with all these qualities of mind and body, Glinton had no heart. No soft sympathies welled up in his bosom for the woes of his fellow-man—no tender yearnings agonised his soul at the misery of another's soul—in vain had "meek-eyed pity" sought an answering echo to her plaintive pleadings—in vain would weeping virtue seek his advocacy—his was not the hand to raise the fallen, to loose the bonds of the afflicted—his were not the eyes seeing for the sightless—his were not the ears hearing for the deaf—his was not the soul that could joy at another's triumph, that could grieve for another's downfall.

Oh! ye ancient wisdom teachers, oh! ye god-men, oh! ye bright-eyed yet venerable sages,—and thou too, thou the muse-loved "blind old man of Scio's rocky isle," were these the lessons you taught—was this the fruit of sacred or of pagan lore?—or of ancient or of modern teaching? Of neither. Breathing truth and wisdom, kindness and intelligence, came ye the ever-living sages,—ye first, by God inspired, glowing with life-fire won from the will of the true Divinity; and ye next, ye too, God inspired (intelligence ever is and must be God's inspiration), veiling beneath pleasing fiction and beautiful imagery all that can elevate, all that can exalt, all that can ennoble mankind. Was it for this that he won the wealthy store, so to misapply the treasure, as one who shall war against a happy nation, only to torture and to enthral its best and bravest.

Was it for this that he read the pages of the past, so to misconstrue their lessons? Not to mention the divine writers, could not those old Grecians with their wondrous tales of valour and of suffering—of philosophy and of mystery—of mind-breathing eloquence and love-fed poetry; could not the olden Roman, gathering and transplanting the Grecian laurels, and telling under their shade his own deeds of patriotism, or rehearsing his own bursts of oratory striving for the right, or his own playful satire, or his love-breathing verse; could not our own country's histories, where, even amid strife and turmoil, some virtue, some valour, ever shines resplendent, even as a diamond irradiating a cavern's depth; could not our own sweet, sweet poesie, always redolent of truth and of tenderness, of energy and of faith—could not the gentle Spenser, or the majestic Milton, or the magic Master of all minds; or could not Italia's vigorous Dante or Petrarch's passioned wooings—nor thine worthy to be princess-loved—could not these—all these—all, as if steeped in heaven's gifts, distilling some good, some blessing; could not these—for with all these he was familiar—win him to sympathy—to affection—to fellow feeling towards his fellow men?

And love too—thou sweet emollient, couldst thou not soften—thou, that now with firm yet gentle force—now with fierce yet not less determined efforts, attackest, assaultest, overcomest what otherwise were impregnable— had'st thou no power? None! there was an antagonist even more powerful—no! not an antagonist, love scorns such an opponent, and quits the contest in contempt and disgust. Selfishness, all-engrossing selfishness, was the gulf that absorbed in Glinton every other thought and sensation—no action, howsoever trivial, but tended to this end—no purpose of his but worked, however remotely, to this intent. I hardly know if selfishness is the term I should have used, if by that term covetousness is inferred, for this was not Glinton's vice, neither was it vanity in its generally received acceptation, for no man could be more indifferent to another's praise, no man more careless of another's censure, than was Forest Glinton. His was that peculiar feeling that wished to make himself the master spirit of every circle wherein he moved, and to subdue or coerce all others' wills to his own, and thence to his advantage. In general he succeeded; almost unknowing it his companions became his subjects—his victims, and though ruled with no lenient sway, few were conscious of the thraldom to which they submitted.

To attain the mastery was ever his object, and for this end no scheme too deep—no simulation too tortuous for him to adopt. Even virtue's fairest outside he could seem to wear, as if it were his habitual garment. "Everything with all men," he appeared to yield to their wishes to the abandonment of his own, while in fact they were placidly following in the track he had selected.

He loved not virtue, nor would he wish others to be virtuous, for he could not deny, even to himself, the superiority, at least inwardly, they must thereby possess over him—internally deriding every feeling, good or pure—internally scoffing at every precept that leads us heavenwards—yet at will he could assume the appearance of being deeply imbued with, and impressed by their

moral and religious lights. Many a youth of the best
and purest principles, listening to his alluring discourses,
did not perceive the fine-spun web of sophistry with
which he, under the appearance of argument seeking
conviction, instilled into the mind of his auditor doubt,
scepticism, and often infidelity; until too late, trembling
on the verge of vice and destruction, the victim wondered how he had been led to the precipitous gulf
he saw no hope of avoiding. Then would Glinton
chuckle to himself at the ruin he had made, and with a
sardonic sneer seek for another victim whose fair fame
seemed to mock his own moral turpitude.

To be superior to Glinton in any one qualification, or
in any of the fortuitous distinctions of life, was to incur
his hatred. There were many, in fact, most of his
associates, men of common and ordinary calibre, with
them he was sufficiently friendly—using them, it is true,
as his tools, appropriating, almost as a favour to themselves, their purses and their attentions—with them he
would unbend into playful satire, frivolity, debauch, or
licentiousness—scenes in which he could best maintain
his superiority over their congenial minds ; and still in
these he contrived ever to uphold his ascendancy and
to receive their homage and their tribute. But roused
once into energy by opposition—thwarted in his will by
determination—then woke the demon in his soul—then,
with rage concealed, or smiling, willing " to murder
while he smiled," he nerved into action every spring
that should minister to his intention.

Divested of any thought save of self, careless or
indifferent how his purpose might affect others, there
was no difficulty he would not overcome, no feelings
that could deter him. His mind, Proteus-like, could

assimilate to all, and cunningly he " bided his time "—
never using force, but mostly stealthily gliding like an
under-current darkly beneath a flowering surface, he
seldom failed to procure sorrow to his opponent, or to sing
his "*Io Triumphe*" over the ruined heart of his victim.

These features of his character continued in after life,
save that he evinced a more decided disposition profita-
bly to avail himself of the advantages which his natural
or acquired superiority over his associates enabled him
to obtain.   This became the more necessary to him, as,
moving in a more extended circle, he found the limited
income which he derived from his family inadequate
for his requirements.   He was therefore more keenly
alive to maintain his ascendancy, for in the busy waters
of life he found he was not the only Triton preying on
the minnows.   He found also that a deeper veil of
duplicity was necessary to mask his natural traits, and
with a ready aptitude, he glided as if by instinct into
each varied disguise, which few were skilful enough to
penetrate, while, at the same time, few could more
readily distinguish the weak points in another's character, and with ready tact and a dexterous yielding to
those foibles from which the wisest of us are not exempt,
he contrived to ingratiate himself with individuals of
the most opposite dispositions.

Glinton had refused some advantageous prospects of
fellowships at the University that might have secured
him independency, as also a proffered living of some
value, if he would have consented to take orders.   He
thought that a wider field was necessary for his career,
and therefore declining these advantages, he had, from
the time of his quitting college until the period of
which I write, been engaged in perpetual struggles

to support the position to which he aspired. Early shut
from the bustling field of politics by some tergiversa-
tion which the keen-witted minister had detected and
remembered, his sphere of action became comparatively
limited, and it often required the utmost exertions of
his Machiavel mind to maintain the power and influence
he assumed, and to which it must have been marvellous
to himself to find so willing a submission.

It is not to be supposed, that I was acquainted with
these particulars at the period of my first knowing the
subject of their details. It was not until after a long
course of dear-bought knowledge, assisted by the
observations and the bitter experience of others, that I
was enabled to form the true estimate of this man's
character.

Our acquaintance commenced, as nearly as I recollect,
in the following manner. The weather being clear and
almost calm, a group, of which I formed one, had assembled on the deck, and after discussing varied subjects,
had gradually fallen into one in which I could not avoid
taking a lively interest. The conversation was on
foreign travel.

"It is a singular thing," observed one of the party,
"that many English, who seek for pleasure in beholding beautiful scenes and picturesque views in other
countries, are entirely unaware of the rich varieties
offered within their native land. But this is not the
only contrariety in society; we find our choicest native
productions despised and neglected, while we admire
and imitate those of our foreign neighbours."

"And as an addition to your remarks," added my
friend, "let me observe how very many who are con-

versant with every detail of information as to foreign
climes and distant ages, are nearly if not totally ignorant of their own country's worthies, and to whom the
history of their own forefathers is as a sealed book."

"From that reproach," observed a voice, almost
musical, "allow me to exempt the Jews; there is no
nation more deeply imbued with the knowledge of their
own history, or more sincerely venerating the eventful
lives of their own ancestors. It is true that they have
a double impetus for this, for associated as their religion
is with their history, it becomes a concomitant necessity
that the study of the one should accompany the study
of the other."

With a look of grateful thankfulness I turned
towards the speaker, and saw a young gentleman, as I
have described Mr. Glinton. Our glances met, and I
am sure he must have observed my enthusiastic look
of gratification, though, dropping his eyes modestly
to the ground, he seemed almost ashamed of having
interfered in the conversation, which now became
general.

"I do not agree with you," observed one of the
former speakers. "I have always heard of the Jews,
that, beyond a few leading facts, they are ignorant of
their own history; that they observe peculiar customs
without being aware of their origin; that they cele-
brate remarkable anniversaries without a knowledge of
the events they commemorate, so that, uninformed
themselves, they are with shame compelled to confess
their inability of imparting to others the information
so often sought for at their hands."

I was about replying rather indignantly, knowing
the utter groundlessness of the charge, but the white

hand of Glinton gently repressed me, and in his mild voice he asked—

"Have you known many Jews?"

"God forbid!" was the answer, with a shrug of the shoulders.

"Then, Sir, I have, and can assure you your impressions are incorrect. Few, even among the very inferior classes, that have occasion to blush on account of the ignorance you impute to them — ignorance which, indeed, would be disgraceful to them — to them the chosen heritors of records of divine inspiration — to them the guardians of the annals of time's infancy, of religion's birth, and the nurslings of philosophy, of the advance of science, and the spread of civilisation."

"Do you mean to assert that the Jews—the scorn of the world—the outcast of nations—"

"Yes, they are scorned, but in the day of their avenging where will be their scorners? outcast—yes they are outcast—but they shall become God's chosen instruments of conquest. I tell you, as a learned writer has said before me, that I never look on one of this despised and persecuted race but in him I behold a living instance of God's power; I never see a poor earth-trodden Israelite, even in the humblest avocation, but in him I see the descendant of a mighty people— mighty in its heroes and its sages—mighty in its prophets and its poets. Sir, in the Jew is a mine of wealth, and they who seek shall find the store."

"Come away, my dear," said a short and rather rubicund visaged lady to the first speaker; "this gentleman is no doubt largely indebted to the Jews, and he seeks to repay part of the obligation."

This was said with a meaning glance at myself.

"I am indeed somewhat indebted to the Jews, even in the sense you imply, Madam," said Glinton, with a bland smile; "but I am under obligations never to be repaid for the enlightenment my mind has received from their histories and their moral code: histories which are the most marvellous as well as the most ancient; moralities which teem with life and love."

"Fine words, fine words."

"Fine words," interrupted I, for I could no longer be repressed. "Yes, Sir, they are fine words, they are noble words, and thus do I, one of the outcast and the scorned, thank their speaker," seizing, as I spoke, the hand of Glinton, which, in my fervour, I could have carried to my lips. "Fine words; yes, Sir, they are fine words, and no less fine than true. Is not the practice of truth and good feeling inseparably connected with our character and professions? is not the exercise of charity, linking man to man in mutual sympathy, pointed out in every branch of our laws? does not our every precept inculcate the folly of pride or of vainglory, warn against vice and folly, teach us how to avoid temptation to error, to practise patience in adversity, and moderation in prosperity?"

"Come here, my dear," interfered the lady again; "there's quite enough talk about such rubbish."

Her not very docile husband, perhaps out of opposition to this open show of authority, or perhaps because he did not consider the subject "such rubbish," proceeded to contest the point.

"Ha! I recollect," said he, "I once did know a Jew, and well was I cheated by him."

"Admit the fact," replied Glinton; "would you charge the crime of one against the mass? Is this even-

handed justice.   Do we Christians never transgress?
yet you, as do some of our otherwise liberal newspapers,
specially designate and comment on the error of the
Jew, perhaps for its rarity, while too many of our own
misdeeds are silently recorded.   But where is the community that has not some unworthy member?   Admit
your statement as an exception, still I maintain that
the Hebrew morality is the morality of mankind; it is
that principle which teaches an equal justice without
distinction of ranks—which elevates the poor to the
level of the rich—which, in the exercise of its attributes, distinguishes not persons—which would make
mankind truly brethren."

"And," added I, "what did the ancient nations
admire and imitate?   With them military heroism was
often an equivalent to all other virtues.   Need I recall
the Spartan encouragement to theft, or the father
sanctioning treachery in the son as a means of gaining
a city, or the classic mother watching with indifference
her last child bleeding on the bier?   Shall I call to
memory the good citizen banished because he was "the
just" or great Plato's master, dying on account of his
many virtues?   Shall I tell you how with them prosperity was ever a licence to luxury, and adversity to
despair?"

"True, the ancients did these things, but were the
favoured people exempt from crime? were they im-
maculate?"

"I do not assert it; many a crime was done among
them, for which they were deservedly punished.   But
with them crimes were not dignified to virtues to be
held up to admiration and imitation."

"Let me also remark," chimed in my ingenious supporter, "on their theocratic form of government, by whose laws even an improper thought was often deemed equal to an improper deed, which curbed every unlawful desire; when even to wish for the property of another was equally culpable with theft. These laws put checks not only on men's conduct, but also on their opinions. It is this peculiar feature of their legislation which has ensured the admiration of every thinking mind. It is this stamp of divine intelligence that has secured, not merely the attention of the theologian but the wonder of countless ages."

"Your argument is good, I admit; but it's getting near dinner time—yes, yes, very convincing—but upon my honour this keen air gives me quite an appetite—yes, yes, quite conclusive—there's the steward, I declare—all very true, no doubt—yes, my dear, I'm coming;" and now, nothing loth, he took the arm of his better half, intent to discuss more solid food than unsubstantial words.

Many more followed the example, and the deck was almost untenanted. Drawing nearer to me, Glinton resumed the conversation. "I have to apologise," said he, "for acting as champion in a cause where you had the best right to be defender, but truly I did not at first know that a Hebrew was present, and I owe too many obligations to the works of your sages ever to allow one of their nation to be reviled without taking up the cause as my own."

"You have studied our literature," said I, with some surprise.

"Yes, and well were my labours repaid. When at Oxford I was engaged in rather abstruse enquiries as to the supposed originals of some of the mystic classical legends, as well as of the mythological system of the ancients. My attention was directed of course to the Scriptures, and necessarily to the commentaries."

" Which you read in the original ? "

" In the original," replied he, smiling at my wonder.

" And the result of your enquiries ? " asked I, for of all subjects, I loved to talk of this, our time-honoured literature.

"In most points satisfactory and conclusive. I have therein traced the germ of many a pagan rite or northern legend ; I have seen how many a mystery of mythology shone but as a scintillation of the attributes of the unknown God. I have recognised amid the fables of Hindoo cosmogony, and amid the chaos of Greece's old antiquity, but a shadowing of God's own creation. The blissful state of our first parents ' ere sin could blight, or sorrow fade,' is the prototype of the poets' age of gold, while the serpent contest and man's prophesied crushing of the reptile teem in varied forms in every clime. Singularly, too, the names of the first mortal pair are preserved in the Sanscrit religious chronicles, and I have found their attributes ' first produced' and 'life '* strangely coincident with the Hebrew original, in a Grecian translation from the Phœnician historians. How clearly is the flood of Deucalion a reflex of the mighty outburst of God's tremendous wrath ! The tripartite division of the universe between Jupiter, Neptune, and Pluto, what is it but the division between the sons of the favoured Noah ? Your Tubal-cain is evidently the original of Vulcan, and his sister (perhaps ' soror et conjux ') Na-amah, which I believe you render

---

* Protogenes and Eon.

' pleasant'; may she not have been the first embodying of the most pleasant goddess ? Your Tower of Babel's rebellious defiance is probably the first idea of the Titan war against Olympus, for ' there were giants in the earth at that time and also after then.' The labours of Hercules, are they not an amplified version of the labours of Sampson, even to the enthralling of the strong man by the luscious but empoisoned draughts of beauty? The immolation of Iphigenia is identical in deed as verbally with Jephtha-genia or daughter. Pylades and Orestes are the shadows of David and Jonathan. I might mention numerous instances in the Hindoo annals—in the Mexican traditions—in the Runic Sagas, or the poetic polytheism of the old Grecians, which are founded on or incorporated with the records and truths of the Hebrews."

" But our great lawgiver, to whom will you assimilate him ? "

" For him I have no similitude ; none but himself can be his parallel. I believe with a perfect faith," continued he, quoting from Maimonides, " that the prophecies of Moses our instructor, were true, and that he excelled any of the sages who preceded him, or who may succeed him."

" You are evidently interested in the Jewish histories," observed my friend.

" Who that is engaged in the details of past ages but must be so. If we seek acquaintance with the history of the Assyrian, the Babylonian, the warlike Persian, or the luxurious Mede, we find them interwoven with facts and allusions which the Hebrew historians can elucidate and explain. But of all these nations, the Assyrian—the Babylonian—the warlike Persian, or the luxurious Mede, what bears the earth of their remembrance?—which of their descendants shall trace the records of their bygone glories, or shall say, 'here my fathers triumphed'? As a tale of forgotten love, there is none to speak of it—none to weep for the ashes of the past. Where is the 'sacred band' now?

"Foreign eyes in foreign lands read their histories—no kindred sympathy is impulsed for their joys or their afflictions—we own no brotherhood with their wisest or their best."

"But we Israelites are not so," said I with enthusiasm—"we remember."

"Can ye forget? Among the wreck of nations ye have outlived the tempest—ye look with affection on your early history, for each noble deed is one of your own ancestry's—ye can join in a patriotic voice in each chorus of triumph—ye can wander to your forefathers' land and trace each scene of valour and of worth. Oh! how I envy even the meanest of your race, imbued as you all must be with the spirit of your faith—entering with devotion into the holiest of mystery! What joy can be so delightful as to imagine the father and the little child, the mother and her dark-eyed daughter, with one accord, reading and fondly commenting in that original volume, and in that self-same language which time has consecrated, and which inspiration has hallowed! What ecstasy so delicious as that when on your holy sabbath eve the parent blesseth his beloved ones in the time-hallowed aspirations of your revered patriarch?"

Borne away by the torrent of his eloquence, I had little power, or, in fact, little wish to interrupt him. Our conversation was prolonged, and its issue was my earnestly and eagerly soliciting the acquaintance of its able supporter. Bound to Paris as well as myself, he promised occasional visits at his disengaged intervals.

Will it be credited, that ably as Glinton had spoken, warmly and enthusiastically as he had maintained his position—will it be credited that he was totally indifferent on the subject. Well acquainted with the details he certainly was—but the warmth with which he spoke of them was artificial—his energy was but as an outward garb. Why, then, so eager in the argument? asks the reader.

Oh! deep and designing, mighty master of man-craft, could he not behold in me one of Israel's sons—had he not heard some remarks where my soul had spoken—did he not seek to win my favour—and oh! deep and designing, did he not know he sought the readiest and the safest path to obtain it.

I anticipate my after-knowledge of motives and events, which of course I could not know at the period of their occurrence—nor, indeed, would I have believed them if then revealed to me.

My friend Frank obtained an earlier insight into his character; indeed, having no purpose to gain in acquiring the friendship of a younger son, he occasionally disdained the forms of disguise, and thus unwarily displayed to Frank's awakened perception, deformities, where to me appeared only beautiful symmetry.

——o——

TO MISS LEONORA DE ROTHSCHILD,

ON THE OCCASION OF HER MARRIAGE.

E lo mie rime
Che son vili e neglette, se non quanto
Coster LE ONORA co'l bel nome santo.
                                    TASSO.

And my rhymes
Worthless and poor, save inasmuch as she
Of her most holy and enchanting name
Does them THE HONOUR.—HOOLE.

UNEXAMPLED worth would Tasso's lyrics praise,
Graceful " Leonora" prompts his votive lays ;
Leonora ! honour's symbol ! spotless name,
Borne on time's pinions, wreathed in purest fame.
D'Esté's fair princess, of principles sublime,
Lives through all ages—triumphs over time.
Though beaming bright in nature's loveliness,
Beauty for her no value did possess,
Save that the light that lit her wondrous face,
Lustrous to virtue gave an added grace.
Shrinking from praise, so walked this noble maid,
Veiling her goodness with a modest shade.
Thus true-born worth to noblest acts allied,
Admired by all, yet seeks from praise to hide.
So she, fair princess, sole on good intent,
More noble by her deeds than proud descent.

And blessed parallel—well with prescient skill,
Who knew her name would her best worth instil;
Prophetic powers, thy parents seem to share,
When her loved name they bade their infant bear.
In childhood—youth—in blossomed life—we see
HONOUR's best symbol glorified in thee;
And all Italia's princess bids us praise,
Revives new-born to bless our happy days.
Have we not seen thee, like an angel bright,
Cheering the drooping—making darkness light?
Have we not heard thee, when, with constant care,
To breathe the improving spirit—righteous there—
Poured forth the treasures of thy well stored mind,
While clustering childhood heard thy words refined?
But why recount what thousand echos speak;
The poor, they bless thee—my best words are weak;
The poor, they bless thee—their voice has reached to
        heaven,
And now to thee, thy best reward is given.

Sweet love by friendship mellowed into bliss;
Is there a joy approximates to this?
A kindred tie, where mutual hopes combine,
A copious store of love's best harvest, thine.
Each thought new-framed—each end the wish dictates,
With winning fondness at thy bidding waits.
Now, doubly blessed, while virtue still thy care,
Linked, hand in hand, thy loved with thee will share.

For him, too, Tasso would have nerved his verse;
His deeds of worth, would he, like thine, rehearse.
Congenial souls, who all their thoughts employ,
Seeking their own, when seeking mankind's joy.

"Jerusalem delivered," well the poet sings,
(Still on fair Venice' lakes the echo rings,)
Soldiers and martyrs, striving in the fight,
Gemmed with fresh valour, gleam with added light.*
But yet, alas! amid th' ennobled tide,
Earth's baser impulse—envy, wrath, and pride,
Motives degenerate noble aims disgraced,
And stained the standard rashly they embraced.

Not so *his* efforts who by faith impelled,
Valiant in purpose, other thoughts repelled.
While holy ardour anxious zeal inspires,
He leaves the home of hope and fond desires ;
For Zion's wall, where tottering age doth creep,
And sainted pilgrims near its ruins weep ;
Where still oppression rules with iron hand,
Crushing with despot grasp the trembling band :
For these he strove—for these he raised the voice ;
And bade the sunken spirits yet rejoice ;
Indolence—fell monster, oft with fear allied—
He stern repelled—with industry supplied ;
New vigoured strength he bids their limbs employ,
And " those who sowed in tears now reap in joy " ;
The land will teem, from apathy set free,
" Jerusalem delivered " best then by thee.

And well repaid, " his bread cast on the waters,"
Art thou not his—thou best of Judah's daughters ?
Loved child of God—thou fair—thou promised land,
Art thou not his ? What more can man demand ?

* " The Crusaders."

——o——

HYMN FOR A DAY OF RELIGIOUS CONFIRMATION.

WITH grateful heart and gladsome voice
    The votive hymn we raise,
Responsive doth each soul rejoice,
    The Rock of Life to praise.

Each springing day, each new-born hour,
    Each moment's transient space,
Bids all creation own His power,
    And glorify His grace.

Life's each extreme, the aged, the child,
    The anxious reverent youth,
The matron sage, the maiden mild,
    One-voiced proclaim His truth.

And chiefly we, who clustered here,
    Like those round Sinai's mount,
His sacred Law well pleased revere,
    His wondrous deeds recount.

O God! who watched our infant course,
    Our onward life secured,
Who nerved our limbs with vigorous force,
    Whose love has e'er endured.

Led by whose will, religious light
    Illumed our inmost soul,
And guided by whose radiance bright,
    This day we reach the goal.

Here, in this sacred house, we stand,
  Here Israel's faith profess,
Here raise we now th' imploring hand,
  O God! our purpose bless.

With anxious zeal and careful thought,
  We strove thy law to know,
With earnest hope our minds have sought,
  In righteous paths to go.

Convinced—we seek this day Thy fane,
  Convinced—our faith declare,
Thy will shall still our guide remain,
  Thy law our constant care.

To love and truth and righteous deeds,
  Each act and word we vow,
Deign Thou, O God! our life to bless,
  For ever then as now.

———o———

THE JEWS AND THEIR ASSAILANTS.

זרים אומרים אין תוחלת ותקוה

" Strangers say there is no expectation nor hope."

They say we have no country now—they taunt us with
  our name;
They *will* not see, in glory's wreath, our brightest branch
  of fame;
They wear the veil of prejudice, to shade their dazzled
  sight

From Judah's blaze of brilliancy—from proud Israel's
    light.

Who are these men of yesterday, that dare malign our
    name?

Would strip us of our royal robes, and cast us forth
    to shame?

Who are these men that nod the head, and pout the
    lip of scorn,

Because they think that Jacob, now, is stricken and
    forlorn?

They cannot see the hidden soul, the latent warmth that
    glows,

That animates 'mid all our gloom—that cheers through
    all our woes.

How can they know, who spurn our race, the patriot
    fire we feel;

Our ardent search for truth and love—our never dying
    zeal?

Why need we tell, all time can speak, our valour and
    our worth;

Why need we fear, when heavens praise, the mockery
    of earth?

Who are these puny cavillers—ephemera of an hour?

What is their boasted pomp and pride, their nothing-
    ness of power?

The envious crew, who fain would rob our shield of
    ancient date

Of all the rich emblazonings they cannot emulate.

A mighty nation ours was then, when e'en their name
    was not;

A mighty nation still will be, when e'en their name's
    forgot.

From heaven's rays our guiding light, before their faint
    spark shone;

Our guiding light from heaven still, their feeble meteor
    gone.
Well, let them rail: they strut and vaunt, yet crouch
    and kiss the rod;
Ours are the men of old renown, the noblemen of God!
Of warriors' deeds, our sages' lore, what need have we
    to boast?
Old time has been our chronicle, the world has seen
    our host;
Has seen that host, first reared in faith, illuminate
    mankind;
Has seen that band dispensing light—forsooth! they
    call us "blind!"
Yes; "blind" are we, that will not see earth's exhala-
    tions guide;
By heaven's orb we steer our course, the vapoury flame
    deride.
So, taught to seek empyreum's height, the eagle, king-
    bird flies;
He, too, is "blind" (?)—that royal bird—owl's twilight
    to despise.

Perverting right, and strangling truth, calumniators
    flock,
Israel's pangs rejoiced to flout—at Zion's throes to mock.
O glorious deed! it well beseems, who envy us our
    name,
With tainted breath to dim our shield, and think they
    blight our fame.
The tempest wind has laid us low, the raging storm
    has past;
Prostrate, contrite, at Heaven's will, we bend us to the
    blast;

Our glorious land is wasted now, our splendid fanes are
    dust;
We bow the head in reverence before the Wise, the Just.
Our slaughtered youth and martyred age have perished
    by the sword,
Unhallowed feet have dared profane the Temple of the
    Lord;
And still we bear our punishment, while stranger chil-
    dren flock,
And puerile men of yesterday at ancient sages mock.

Oh! for the time, the glorious time! we patiently await,
When crouching men, who now deride, shall stand at
    Zion's gate;
The nations then, with trembling awe, will clutch
    Israel's skirt—
The mockers *now*, the tremblers *then*—their ruin to
    avert.
Lebanon *then*, a fruitful mount, that now is drear and
    waste,
Shall shade the crowd of suppliants that round her
    cedars haste,
The humbled proud, the mighty weak, in Salem's light
    to live;
Israel's glad revenge shall be, to pity and forgive.
Oh! for that day of triumph; oh! for that blissful time,
To shield the men who spurn us now, in God's own
    sacred clime;
To hear them say, who jeer us now—repentingly—
    mankind,
Their souls have lived, defying death; we could not
    slave the mind.
O joy! O joy! when once again we tread that sacred
    soil,

We press the vine of fruitful hills, and Gethsemene's
    oil;
And Gilead too distils her balm, and vale and mount
    rebound
The echoed notes of gladness then, that through the
    land resound.
The time will come, O Judah, rouse! to share this proud
    estate,
Awake! arise! despise the gibes of envy, scorn, and
    hate:
By energy and active good we'll all their spite defy,
By energy and active good we'll give our foes the lie.
Remember your ancestral deeds—the fame your fathers
    won;
Be this your noblest pride, to be those fathers' worthy
    son;
And when, the tide of lifetime o'er, we bid this world
    adieu,
Be this our noblest epitaph, " He lived and died a Jew."

---o---

THE POOR FRUIT BOY.

HE dared not beg, he would not steal;
No friend to help him to a meal,
    To work he was too weak;
His mother sick, his father dead,
His little sister wanting bread,
    Pale woe was on each cheek.

One single shilling all their store ;
Save that they could not hope for more ;
   A scanty hope for three.
And there they sat in commune sad,
That sickly mother, child, and lad,
   Of what their course might be.

A thousand thoughts did each disclose,
A thousand fond devices rose,
   Like fairy visions wild ;
Till with a smile, as near to glee
As could 'mid pinching famine be,
   Out spoke the little child.

O! mother, love! my counsel hear,
Give all we have to brother dear,
   With that he fruit shall buy,
God's blessing on his labours be,
With store of profit soon shall he
   Our every want supply.

The sanguine mother kissed her child,
One moment of her cares beguiled,
   And turned aside to weep ;
The girl, tho' gnawed by hunger's fangs,
To hide from all those piercing pangs,
   Feigned placidly to sleep.

The boy, with anxious hope elate,
Sees brightening forth a happy fate,
   Invests with joy his wealth ;
In each fresh fruit he sees some good,
In this, for sister, store of food ;
   In that, for mother, health.

Alas ! too soon, alas ! for him,
His visioned brightness fading dim,
　　He fronts the Justice Seat,
Condemned—in Britain's boasted clime ;
Since when is industry a crime ?
　　Is Justice' self a cheat ?

The trembling boy, with weeping eyes,
His sentence hears with sad surprise ;
　　One thought soon fills his mind ;
O ! who shall ease his mother's grief,
To hungry sister bring relief,—
　　To prison he's consigned.

Well pleased, content, the magistrate
Now hastens home with joy elate,
　　He has his duty done.
His wife, with glee, returns his smile ;
His children they with sports beguile,
　　How sweet the bright hours run !

The well stored plate, the choicest wine,
And all to tempt his taste combine ;
　　Each " dainty cate " is there ;
The good man pats his well filled vest,
And breathes before he sinks to rest
　　To mercy's God a prayer.

The widowed mother, she, too, prays ;—
Five nights and five long anxious days,
　　Her heart nigh bursts with grief.
The girl, more happy, sinks in death ;
The boy returns, a lie each breath,
　　A prison-nurtured thief !

O God! O God! is this Thy doom?
Thy venging might and power resume,
  Let loud Thy thunders speak.
Not these the laws that Heaven made,
Not this the voice of Him who bade
  Protect the poor and weak.

———o———

A LOVE-LETTER.

TO H——.

(WRITTEN CON-AMORE.)

WILL you, love, complain, if changing my strain, I seek
to amuse in this letter; and though I indite, in haste
as I write, I would that the wording were better. Yet
e'er has it chanced, when most I'd advanced, and
wished most my skill to display, the words I would
speak, were faulty and weak, "like fairy dreams melting away." How often the heart, that pants to impart,
the depth of its deep-treasured love, finds eloquence
fail, and truth not avail (the raven outflieth the dove.)
So falsehood full oft—dark, glossy, yet soft—pours forth
in rhetorical flight; nor pauses, nor falters, its swift
speed ne'er alters—though raven-hued, darksome as
night. But truth, like the dove, o'erburdened with
love, that knows not a thought of dissembling, with
timorous wing—though upward she spring—like Noah's
bird feeble and trembling. But ah! happy thought,
just e'en as *she* brought, the olive's bright emerald leaf,
though weak is my flight, it pierces the night—once
more in the ark ends my grief. Thou, love, art the

K

Ark, with thee I embark, and care not for storm or for flood. Wild waters were raging, no hope was assuaging, gone, gone, were each floweret and bud ; my soul like the ocean, in restless commotion, with tempest and whirlwind was tossed ; each thought of hope banished, each joy of life vanished, all earthly enjoyments were lost. No voice rose to cheer me, a friend was not near me, I lived in the world's crowd alone ; fatigued with enduring, my woes seemed past curing, my heart was fast changing to stone. My soul's best physician—my life's brightest vision—came winning me back from despair ; came rousing and cheering, came fondly endearing,— came, bliss, life, and hope to declare. Oh ! bless'd the desiring, oh ! bless'd the acquiring, oh ! bless'd was thy dearest consenting, oh ! joy to behold thee, oh ! bliss to enfold thee, my fondest of wishes contenting. *Now* life is worth living—now love is worth giving— now saved from the turbulent billow ; in calm recollection, thy guardian affection throws haloes of light o'er my pillow. The day glides in gladness, untainted by sadness, thy form is for ever before me ; in fancy I press thee, in joy I caress thee, in holy love bless and adore thee.

The night is advancing, the pale moon is glancing, and nature seems sunk in repose, and I am now musing, how you, dear, are using, the time that so tardily goes. Of me are you thinking ? ere slumber is sinking, with leaden weight closing your eyes ; or chance in your dreaming, you fondly are scheming, the future in brightest of dyes. Bright, glorious Elysian, the joyous glad vision, that lights up thy soul in thy slumber ; far, far, be the feelings, the saddened revealings, the pathways of life that encumber.

And so may our union—blessed in communion—like spring-tide embroidered with flowers, be fragrant and blooming, each new day resuming, an increase of life's brightest hours. Away every trouble—we'll joyous redouble endeavours each other to please; and each one confessing, each other a blessing—each other a comfort and ease.

——o——

TO A FAIR CRITIC,

CONDEMNING ONE OF THE AUTHOR'S PRODUCTIONS

(NOT HEREIN INSERTED).

You blame me that I write in strains,
    Where passion rolls in wildest flood;
Where vice but shows her darkening stains,
    And virtue withers in the bud.
You blame me that I bare a heart,
    Base as the world had e'er engendered,
Where Heaven claims no kindred part,
    And only demon thoughts are tendered.
"False to nature," still you cry,
    "The wretched soul your pen depicted;"
And from the hateful tale you fly,
    As if its sounds some pang inflicted.
Oh! Lady, passing on in life,
    With mind all pure, and heart untainted,
You little know the tale of strife
    On human canvas is empainted.

You little guess the rackened pangs,
   Wrung from withered woes' o'erstraining;
You never saw foul passion's fangs,
   Nor heard the conscience mute complaining.
When vice came decked in virtue's garb,
   And with insidious tones was stealing,
Till rankling now with poisoned barb,
   Too late unmasked the fiend's concealing;
And mingled venom in the veins,
   Changes every noble feature,
No healthy feeling now remains,
   But man becomes a fallen creature;
And all the treasured ties we love,
   The mercy-streams of hope and truth,
Proud aspirations from above,
   Bright evergreens of springing youth;
Affection's fond and holy greeting;
   Obedience to a will divine,
Words, and hearts, and deeds still meeting,
   In homage at a godly shrine;
And life that might have flown so purely,
   Like foretastes of a Heaven's beaming,
The proud soul treading on securely,
   For all around but light is gleaming.
You never saw the saddened wreck
   Of this enriched and noble freighting,
When waves rushed o'er the parting deck,
   And death the fated crew awaiting.
Oh! look you on the rock-fixed hull,
   Hushed is the roaring ocean-demon;
The storm has settled in a lull—
   Where are the gallant stalwart seamen?

And look again, the valued bark
　　Is crusted all around with living,
Foul creatures, mingled mass of dark,
　　No glimpse of former glories giving.
You ne'er had deemed when anchor weighing,
　　Elate with joy, the crew were singing,
How soon upon that deck were preying,
　　Sea monsters, thousand arms outflinging.
Man's mind the wreck, where all forgotten,
　　The cargo sunk, the seamen perished ;
Yet on the planks now damp and rotten,
　　Ten thousand horrid forms are cherished.

———

'T is not because you daily see
　　Around you only virtue brightening ;
And all your kindred seem to be
　　Pure lamps of Heaven's own enlightening,
That you should doubt of naphtha bubbling,
　　From darkened soil unhallowed fire ;
Oh ! could you see the soul's entroubling,
　　The maniac heart, the shattered lyre ;
Blights that give the life a tainting,
　　Scatt'ring all its bright exhale,
Tinging o'er with saddened painting,
　　Turning all its joy to wail ;—
Could you trace the onward rushing
　　Of hopes descending to despair,
When cheeks that once were crimson blushing,
　　Now only seek in crime to share ;—
Could you see pure faith's annulling,
　　Blasted in pestif'rous breath,
Flowers you were this moment culling,
　　Wither in a wasting death ;-—

The thought you were so fondly prizing,
 That still with strength thro' danger buoyed,
Could you feel that " one " despising,
 The chambers of the heart home void,
The madness, anguish, grief and sin,
 The misery, wretchedness and woe ;
How speedily fell vice will win,
 O'er e'en the fairest forms below ;—
You had not deemed my strain too rude,
 Nor passion all too strongly tinted ;
'Tis well when in our solitude,
 The mind is but with good emprinted.

'Tis gloom yet while these lines I write,
 Thou sleepest on in happy dreaming ;
God keep thee still in virtue's light,
 God's guarding love around thee gleaming.

AIDS TO REFLECTION.

(AN EPIGRAM.)

At sacred facts you mock and jeer,
 All marvellous deeds you scout,
Affect a supercilious sneer ;
 You criticise and doubt.

The serpent and the speaking ass
 Awake your curt objection ;
The hours you stand before your glass
 Do they bring no reflection ?

SLEEPING AND WAKING.

" O sleep! gentle sleep, how have I affrighted thee,
That thou no more wilt weigh my eyelids down,
Nor steep my senses in forgetfulness."

SHAKSPEARE.

I DREAD to sleep—for then remembered themes
　　In brightened tints as in that happy time,
　　When cherished hopes just budded in their prime,
Rush o'er my restless couch in vivid dreams;
And then again I live that life of love,
　　And from her lips repeated blisses taste,
　　And clasp again that gently yielding waist,
And envy not the joys of heaven above.
Thus nightly o'er my conscious fancy gleams,
　　While once again in fond embrace we meet,
　　And once again in bliss our pulses beat,
Remembrance of those bright but vanished dreams:
　　Then while I haste her proffered hand to take
　　The vision fades—and then, I dread to wake.

I dread to wake—for then my thoughts will stray,
　　And sad I feel, and drear and desolate,
　　And then I brood upon my hapless fate,
O'er which no hope-beams shed a cheering ray.
Elate with joy, though now so lowly thrown,
　　What bitterness the live-long day to think,
　　That life to me is but an endless link,
A chain of woe that drags my spirit down.

So liko a forest treo the bolt has blighted,
　　That though the trunk remains, the pith has gone,
　　Even in desolation my mind thinks on,
Upon those verdant hopes my soul delighted.
　　Heart's ruins round thus memory's ivies creep—
　　With these my waking thoughts I dread to sleep.

I dread to sleep—for busy dreams recall,
　　And then I shudder while again I seo,
　　Starting renewed in fancy's imagery,
That fatal hour, my life-time's funeral.
Then words are said which pierco my soul to hear,
　　And hands are raised to bar mo from her sight,
　　And worst of all, I see the maddoning blight,
Lovo changed to hate, and sparkling smile to sneer.
Had this dread sight, indeed, boon only seeming,
　　Liko nightly dreams had day deeds never been,
　　Such fatal misery had I never seen,
Elysium still my life had e'cr been beaming.
　　Now, night or day, my heart but throbs to ache,
　　And then I dread to sleep—I dread to wake.

————o————

A LIBEL.

" Your brother has said I've the voice of a crow,
　　And my features resemble an ox;
He may find mo to deal with a troublesome foe,
　　If again thus my person ho mocks."

" I think, my dear Sir, your informant is wrong,
　　So much of my brother I know,
For the animal race his regard is so strong,
　　He'd not libel an Ox or a Crow."

קול רנה וישׂועה :

"A VOICE OF SONG AND SALVATION."

INSCRIBED TO SIR MOSES MONTEFIORE, ON THE 20TH ANNIVERSARY
OF THE OPENING OF HIS SYNAGOGUE AT RAMSGATE.

Who shall aspire?   The holy task who dare?
A fitting house of God, whose hands prepare?
"The heaven of heavens cannot contain His praise,"
Then who on earth His sanctuary may raise?
What motives rare should in that man combine,
Whose pious heart suggests this grand design;
What impulse guide—what faith his mind pervade,
Whom virtue prompts, and heaven's dictates aid?

In ancient times, this fond desire we trace,
To rear to God some sacred worship-place,
Whether as humble altar—gorgeous shrine,
Alike in purpose—holy—blessed—divine!
E'en so did pious Abram altars raise,
Where'er he wandered in his devious ways;
At Moreh, Hebron, Bethel (house of God),
Displayed his faith where'er his footsteps trod;
Transcendant, then, his truth's triumphant test,
Moriah's mount, the patriarch's zeal confessed.
And mark we well, he best his God doth serve,
Who best for man doth kindly love preserve;
Who nerves the weak, who generous aid extends,
And prompt, when danger calls, protects—defends!

Through stranger lands, when Jacob onward pressed,
Humbly at Bethel hear the heart's request:
"Be thou my guide, whereto my footsteps roam,
Be thou my help; in peace, oh bring me home!"
With grateful thanks, the reverent Jacob view,
At holy Bethel, votive vows renew,
To Him, the guardian God, who succour sent,
Whose mercy shielded whereso'er he went.

When rescued hosts went forth from Egypt's land,
Well pleased, free-hearted men heard God's command;
And bounteous gifts were brought with one accord,
To grace the Tabernacle—"holy to the Lord."
Then Israel's children fashioned true and well,
The consecrated home where He might dwell;
Where they might flock with faith and trust replete,
And there their Father-God be sure to meet.
With zeal intent, with holy purpose fraught,
"E'en as the Lord commanded, Moses wrought."*
The noble chief, the perfect work confessed,
And then, with pious love, the people blessed.

Yet pause we not, though lengthened lists proclaim,
Who structures raised, where blessed His sacred name.
Search Scripture's page, and mark the wise and true,
With ardent zeal, this sainted work renew;
Ascending still, till now, the climax won,
One fabric towers—'tis thine, King David's son!
"Beauty's perfection," "Joy of all the earth,"†
Thy wisdom, Solomon, there displayed its worth.
But not thy affluent store of Eastern gold,
Nor gorgeous wealth the eye did there behold,

* Exodus xxxix. 43. † Lament. ii. 15.

Nor cedar'd shafts, nor matchless works of art,
Was half so glorious as thy humble heart,
When prostrate, in thy temple, lowly there,
In soul-felt eloquence, streamed thy noble prayer.
Nor all thy choristers, warbling notes divine,
Woke half the harmony, heaven loves, like thine,
Around when Israel's congregation stood,
And thou—imploring for thy people's good !*

We pass the hour of Judah's gloom and woe,
Her nation captive, and her temple low.
More joyous theme ! we hail the gladsome sight,
A second temple merges quick to light;
Where Ezra's zeal the people's path directs,
And Nehemiah bold, their faults corrects.
And after these, in every changeful time,
Where Israel roamed through many a varied clime,
Still vivid piety holy works dictate,
The house of prayer, to God they dedicate.

Can modern days no parallel afford,
Of righteous men, who strive to love the Lord?
Who, zeal impelled, the hallowed building raise,
Assembled where our hearts in fervour praise?
Yes! well we know how good example moves,
How prompt the hand in work the soul approves.
So, goodly men, in every age are found,
And sacred fanes in every land abound.
Worthy, like Abram, ONE my verse could name,
Whose deeds will live, imperishable in fame ;
Like Abram, he, by ardent faith impelled,
Strove for the right, and every wrong repelled ;

* 1 Kings viii.

Like Abram, he, with brotherly love imbued,
"E'en to Damascus"* treacherous foes pursued.
Subdued and shamed, the scouted tyrants flee,
The hero joys—his captive brethren free!

Mid glowing heat, or piercing cold, unchanged,
To tend his sheep, the patriarch Jacob ranged;
So too, his flock to shield from harm or ill,
Our guardian strove, unfaltering in his will.
One while to sultry East he wandered forth,
Then braved the frosts of chill and piercing North;
And more, the despot's frown he braved to dare,
In Israel's cause, unknown or fear or care.
Like Jacob, too, he prayed with heart intent,
And God protected wheresoe'er he went;
An angel, guarding, walked thy steps beside,
Thy course to cheer, to animate and guide.

So might we trace, in each similitude,
Some semblance of this man with faith imbued;
Alike in name, alike in holy worth,
Our people's leader wins the praise of earth;
In kindly love he aids his people's cause,
In kindly love promotes our faith and laws;
The sacred dwelling, like his namesake rears,
Where fervid he, eternal might reveres!

Honour and wisdom, right-used wealth, combine,
In him, as Solomon, aiding his design.
Jerusalem, of each, will honoured deeds recount,
Whose bounty flowed 'neath Zion's favoured mount;
Distress assuaged, the needy's want relieved,

* Genesis xiv. 15.

The heart rejoiced, in woe, erewhile which grieved ;
Hope for the hopeless, comfort for the weak,
Of these their deeds doth grateful Zion speak.

As diamonds' light, which way so e'er we turn,
Sparkling in lustre, radiant we discern ;
So, gemmed in him, of various good we see,
" Not one, but many saints' epitome."

Yes ! this the man, who well the task may dare,
A fitting house of God, whose hands prepare.
Well done the task ! the sacred fabric raised !
There many a year, right well hath God been praised ;
With reverent joy is welcomed holy day,
There heartfelt piety heartfelt vows repay ;
Responsive there is heard *her* tuneful voice,
Whose pious echo bids *thy* heart rejoice ;—
Long may she live, thy pleasure and thy pride,
Thy guardian angel, tending by thy side ;
Long years of bliss, be yours, ye happy pair,
Blessed days like *this* be yours long time to share.
Whate'er each wish, that wish perfected be :
" As God with Moses was, so be thy God with thee."*

—o—

WHAT'S IN A NAME ?

(AN EPIGRAM.)

" A NAME that's expressive, my daughter should bear,"
    An " unlicensed practitioner" said ;
" Your remark," cried a wag, " is both prudent and fair,
    So we 'll Charlotte-Ann christen the maid."

* Joshua i. 17.

THE HEBREW GENTLEMAN.

APART from all the sacred fame
  That halos round our hero's story,
Bright deeds of worth and valour claim
  For him a noble wreath of glory.
I speak not now of Abram's zeal,
  His earnest faith in God's divinity,
The impetus that made him feel,
  In new-born spotless pure virginity,
The reason light that woke his soul,
  That dawned expansive o'er his mind,
That crushed the idol's false control,
  And with his every wish combined.

How, proud to do what God decreed,
  He left his long-loved native home,
Unconscious where his course would lead,
  Content, with faith, well nerved to roam.
E'en in that saddened parting hour,
  His heart a kindred love confest,
And thrilled with sympathetic power
  That could not be in all repressed.
One link ere he his home forsakes,
  To shelter, cherish, and protect,
Fondly he now his nephew takes,
  Whose course he would in right direct.

Yet vainly taught by every good,
  His own example best supplied,
In truth and loving brotherhood,
  Lot's course in virtue's path to guide,
When strife and passion uncontrolled,
  Their herdsmen stirred with raging ire,
Here Abram's generous acts behold,
  See peace his earnest, sole desire.
"Leave we," he said, "these fertile plains,
  Choose thou, where'er thy thoughts incline,
What then the land to me remains
  Will I for pasture field design."
The choice, by right, by age, by power,
  Well might the elder kinsman claim,
Yet generous e'en in strife's dark hour,
  He still preserves that noble fame
That stamped his every act of life,
  Where'er his varied course we scan,
With worth and valour ever rife,
  The fine old Hebrew gentleman.

And valiant chief, in battle brave,
  Prompt to contrive—quickly achieve,
Th' ungenerous Lot he hastes to save,
  Nor him a captive slave will leave.
Strategic skill he well displays,
  His force he leads through hazy night;
Victorious sees the dawning rays
  Shine on the hero of the flight.
In serried ranks his valiant troops
  Their peaceful bearing now resume,
Disordered crouch the trembling groups,
  Waiting the vanquished's fatal doom.

The monarch humbled anxious craves,
   Forfeited his subjects' lives,
His right to claim as bondage slaves
   The victor's spoil, the chief derives.
The gold, the wealth, the richest gems,
   The battle's spoil, the conqueror's prize;
The generous chief with scorn contemns,
   And doth each gorgeous garb despise.
And yet with prudent thoughtfulness
   (For self he every gift rejects),
For those who shared his proud success,
   Justly their claims he firm protects.

Triumphant chief, of kings the guest,
   Well might his heart with pride have glowed;
A stronger feeling warmed his breast,
   Calm, modest meekness' loved abode.
Who wise, who true, who rightly good,
   Knew, though himself were robed in light,
That all had not fell vice withstood,
   That some had swerved from paths of right.
For these he wept, for these implored,
   For these invoked the ruth divine,
For these his supplicating word
   Continuous prayed at mercy's shrine.
Not as the hypocrites of earth,
   Who walk in self-donned robes of white,
Wrapped up in self-spun garbs of worth,
   Their failing brother spurn in spite:
Brighter his rays of kindness beam,
   For mankind's good his every plan,
As his, my fond and hopeful theme,
   This true old Hebrew gentleman.

Though seeming light, I deem this phrase
   Characteristic, rightly used,
For him, throughout whose lengthened days
   Each gentle, noble act was fused;
Whose soul in one melodious tone
   In unison attuned to good,
Harmonious echoes oft would own,
   Vibrating where best understood.

See! the way-worn wanderer come,
   Fainting across the desert sands,
Welcome! proffered rest and home,
   And ample food from generous hands;
Sustaining hope, dispelling fears,
   The chieftain hastes his aid to give,
The cheering voice the wanderer hears,
   Again his drooping spirits live.
Before the feeble voice can speak
   Liberal gifts he bounteous proffers,
Sustains the powerless, aids the weak,
   Benevolent his aid he proffers.

Considerate e'en in hour of grief,
   Kindly when sympathising friend,
To give his saddened soul relief,
   Doth willing outstretched hand extend,
The "double cave," though much desired,
   Is gratefully as gift rejected,
But rightly paid the price required,
   At length is willingly accepted.
Unnumbered deeds well might I trace,
   Gemm'd alike with virtue's lustre,
Each filled with some most valued grace,
   Sparkling in a brilliant cluster.

L

But abler pens can better write,
  Of him who first with faith unfurled
The banner of that glorious light
  Which cheers and elevates the world;
For me, I only seek to tell,
  As year to year his course proceeds,
The kindly acts he loved so well,
  The worth that kindred worth succeeds,
The generous impulses that stirred,
  Congenial with his life-blood ran,
Who ever was, in deed and word,
  The true old Hebrew gentleman.

—o—

"WHO GAVE YOU THAT NAME?"

(AN EPIGRAM.)

"My name is none of modern state,
  Like Howard, Percy, Seymour, Stanley;
I claim a far more ancient date,
  More noble, glorious, proud, and manly."

"You're right, my friend, I know the book,
  Records your claim with compeers plenty;
None can dispute who rightly look,
  In Genesis, second, nineteen, twenty."

—o—

JOACHIM HAYMAN.

(A SCHOOL-DAY REMINISCENCE.)

AMONG eighty boys who composed the establishment of our principal, it may be supposed there existed a great diversity of disposition, yet in one particular they all seemed to unite. This was in a desire to tease and annoy one individual lad, who now seemed the butt of their jokes, and now the victim of their capricious tyranny. Joachim Hayman was a Hollander by birth; this alone was sufficient to promote their jibes and jeers; prone as boys and even men are to catch at national peculiarities, it may be supposed that this, the mere circumstance of his birth, would be enough to provoke their observation and comment; add to this Joachim was dull, sluggish, almost an idiot; yet were times when the flash of genius would sparkle forth with a dazzling radiance; though after this ebullition of light, the gloom of his mind then seemed doubly obscure.

Though myself not of the brightest capacity, I was easily tempted to join in this unnatural baiting; and now I wonder how I could so easily, and with such satisfaction, have partaken in this fiendish torture. Then I did not know, or if I knew, did not sufficiently conceive this youth's story—a few words will tell it.

His father had been a wealthy merchant at the Hague, and having acquired a princely fortune, purposed retiring to England, the native country of his wife, to enjoy his opulence. For this purpose he had taken shipping in a homeward-bound merchantman, with his four sons and three daughters, and attended by numerous domestics, who, loth to forsake so kind a master, had obtained permission to accompany him. On the morning when they embarked for Albion's shore, the sky was blue and serene, while a freshening favouring breeze foretold a prosperous voyage. But a sudden and violent tempest too soon belied these flattering hopes; two nights and days the fragile bark was tossed to and fro, the sport of boisterous winds and threatening waves, till at length striking a hidden rock, she filled and sank almost immediately. Of the whole family but Joachim was saved; father, mother, kindred, friends had perished; he was alone in the world. He was picked up in a state of exhaustion by the boat's crew of an English vessel, and being brought to England, was sent by his father's agent to our academy. But the fatal blow had been struck—"reason frighted from her empire" had fled; and the once lively, gay, and happy boy vegetated into the being I have described him. One single, solitary incident seemed to have possession of his imagination, to the exclusion of all others—a confused recollection of a wreck; beyond, all was a blank. He had acquired an imperfect knowledge of English, and by a singular fatality, his sole, his only delight was in perusing narratives of voyages, tempests, and shipwrecks. For hours together, he would sit in a corner of the play-ground, under an old yew tree, his favourite resort, regardless of the practical jokes of his unfeeling tormentors, (a helpless Samson, ministering sport to the Philistines,) absorbed in the all-engrossing themes that fed the fever of his mind; spelling with assiduous diligence the difficult words with which they abounded. Poor fellow! he had asked the boys to read them to him, and they had misguided him. The sea phrases caught his attention, recalled for a time former associations, and were treasured up in the store-house of his memory, as an intellectual feast, with which he would occasionally indulge himself. Of course, unacquainted with their technicalities, they were improperly applied by him; indeed, I much question whether, even theoretically speaking, at this time, he knew the stem from the stern, or any other of the simplest nautical distinctions. Yet have I seen him, even amid the pelting storm, and unconscious of the boisterous merriment that surrounded him, acting, with all the ideal reality of his imagination, and interlarding his actions with oddly assorted phrases, scenes in the life of a mariner. First all joy, animation, and buoyancy weighing anchor; then by a happy imitation, the boatswain's call; heaving the lead; reefing, and furling the sails; manning the yards; the steersman at the helm—the captain on the deck—the mariner in the foretop—the crew's exultation at a prosperous gale. Now he would imagine the wind to change—the clouds to threaten—the sky darkening—the sea-birds screaming, and all the portents of a violent tempest. "Hark! Hark!" he would cry, "to that pealing thunder; see the raging waves that sweep the deck; quick, quick, all hands aloft; reef the top sails; look to the main mast; it shivers in the lightning's flash; stand clear; it falls. Water, water in the hold! All hands to the pumps. Gracious Heavens, a rock on the starboard bow! keep her clear! she strikes! she leaks! Oh God! she sinks!" He would then fall to the ground, and "like a strong swimmer in his agony" would buffet to and fro, till exhausted by his exertions of mind and body, he would remain in a state of torpid inaction.

But a singular circumstance was connected with this delusion of the senses. Though, as I have before stated, attached to nautical descriptions, and employing many of his leisure hours in designing and carving small models of ships and boats, which he really executed with no small degree of tact, they produced no further amusement to him ; he was unable to launch them, as he never could endure the sight of a pool, or any other collection of the aqueous element.* This feeling differed in a certain degree from that experienced by hydrophobial subjects, as water did not affect him when used as a beverage, but merely when having occasion to pass a brook or other running stream, a confused train of ideas would unbidden rush to his recollection, he would relapse suddenly from the highest ebullition of mirth into involuntary tears, and if not restrained, would seek by flight to avoid the uncongenial object. These traits of his disposition did not escape his juvenile tormentors, who let no opportunity pass of indulging their malicious sport. To my shame and sorrow be it spoken, I, from having first through mere thoughtlessness joined this brutal pastime, became eventually the foremost of his assailants, " regardless

---

* Many years after the above was written, in a report respecting the Asylum for Idiots, at Earlswood, I met with the following (See "Times," June 22, 1866.)—"There is another whose drawings sell at high prices, and who has made perhaps the most complete model of a ship that was ever constructed, which he exhibits with justifiable pride, and attempts to describe with great volubility, although scarcely able to utter a word which a stranger can understand."

of wringing or breaking a heart, already to sorrow resigned."

Even Saturday, our Sabbath, our day of rest, was no Sabbath, no resting day to him. Unhappy youth, without a parent's aid to guide him—no home to shelter him—no friend to cheer him.

Yes! one friend he had, a friendship worth a thousand loves: Amelia, thou wert the most meek, the most estimable of women; to thee, as to a resting-place, his wandering spirit yearned amid the troubled waters; and truly thou didst not withhold the branch of grace. Amelia was the niece of our preceptor, adopted by him at the death of her parents from combined motives of humanity and economy; she ranked in his household in the capacity between that of a relation and a housekeeper. Of her fitness for the station I know not, but as it gave her an opportunity of attending to our comfort, which was her studious care, she was a general favourite with the scholars. Of a mild, placid, and contented aspect, the beauties of her countenance seemed veiled with resignation to the humble state in which she had been placed—a virgin lily bending to the storm. She was, at the time of which I have been speaking about seventeen, sylph-like in form, oh! how angel-like in action; pensive as she walked along—timid as a young fawn, and starting even at the echo of her own melody, you would have little guessed the language of those gazelle-like eyes that sparkled beneath their silken fringes. Herself an orphan, she was easily attracted by the ties of sympathy to the yet more friendless Hayman. And the boy felt her kindness; the only smile that lit up his sluggish countenance was at her approach, and if the music of *her* voice

floated from the distance, his dull grey eyes would
gradually unclose their ponderous lids, and sparkle for
a moment with delight. Blessed creature, how often
have I seen you beseeching us, the relentless tyrants of
this hapless orphan, to desist from our unfeeling enjoyment! Nor did you plead in vain—the sound of your
angel voice soothed us to compliance, alas! but for a
time. With me, as being more in her company, she
was more frequent in her beseechings in behalf of the
poor boy, and I, not insensate to the mute language of
tears, that frequently usurped the place of words, made
repeated promises, but again to violate them.

It was a sultry day in July, when Mr. W. desired
the boys to prepare for walking. We were speedily
marshalled and in order, under the superintendence of
one of the teachers, and, after a promenade of some
duration, reached a meadow where was a well-known
brook, that had often tempted our heated frames to
lave in its cooling streams. It was hidden from our
immediate view by a clump of willows, that intercepted
the perspective from the point at which we were approaching. Though often wishing to enjoy the refreshing element, the injunctions of our master were strict
against us, in consequence of some unfortunate accidents; but, in this instance, we hoped to be more
successful, as the usher, whose routine it was to convoy
us, was deeply immersed in the pages of a pocket
Sallust or Virgil, his never-failing companion. He
was a mild, harmless, and inoffensive man; unconscious of his own acquirements, yet of profound
erudition, a very Dominie. A Scotchman too, a Camp-
bell, or a Grant, I forget which, his clan was broken
up, and he wandered forth to live by his knowledge.

Very intellectual was he, even in aspect, not like his co-temporary, the great Colossus, moving under mountain masses of flesh, an imperious tyrant in his domain, but gaunt, tall, meagre-looking, yet placid withal. Polyphemus-like, his single orb sparkling with delight at the discovery of some hidden meaning in the Classics, or some supposed coincidence of Xenophon and Plutarch, or the restoration of a lost line of Eschylus or Euripides. He verily lived on the fruit of the tree of knowledge. A glutton in literature, he devoured with eagerness all within his grasp. Abstemious in diet, parsimonious in expenditure (the vice or virtue? of his countrymen), very, very cleanly in attire, his plain cut suit of grey mixture, his black straw hat, and dark worsted stockings, never varying in appearance, were the outward bark of which the tree was unconscious. He had been at Culloden they said; more from instinct than inclination "he followed to the field his warlike lord," and had escaped with loss of an eye, to retread the more congenial paths of literature.

Such was our English master, and it may be supposed that we boys availed ourselves of his abstraction to enjoy our unrestrained caprices. We had now reached the Rubicon, a simultaneous desire impelled us to rush into the stream, like a caravan of camels at the glad sight of water in the desert. Undeterred by the presence of our teacher, who was now seated under the umbrageous boughs of a venerable oak, immersed in a favourite ecologue, I was rushing among the foremost, when my attention was arrested by an unusual bustle, a confused sound of boisterous merriment, and a voice of lament. Hastening to the spot, I saw poor Hayman in the hands of a knot of young Pharaohs, who were preparing to plunge him in the water, regardless of his well-known and unconquerable aversion to that element. They had already divested him of part of his attire, and one boy, the Hercules of the school for size and might, was endeavouring to snatch from his hold a locket which he had worn, and which Joachim convulsively grasped to retain. "My mother! my mother!" shrieked the poor boy; the first time I had ever heard him mention her. Electrically through my whole frame I felt the force of the appeal; to see and to hear were one impulse; my sudden and violent blow levelled his assailant with the earth; the group, struck with astonishment retreated for a moment, while their victim bounded like a young fawn across the plain, still shrieking as he went, "My mother! my mother!"

From that hour a sudden revulsion of feeling pervaded my whole frame with respect to this youth—a bond of silent sympathy. He, too, had had a mother, whom he had loved, and whom, like me, he had lost, and whose image he fondly cherished. From having been his foremost opponent, I became his firmest friend and protector; and, accustomed as he had been to regard me as his foe and oppressor, he now looked up to me as an ægis, always ready to shield him. And as I was allowed a greater latitude than the other boys, my father's interest being very useful to Mr. W., I was enabled to procure him many advantages, from which he would otherwise have been debarred, and relieved him from those annoyances to which even his hours of rest, falsely so-called, were subjected.

Amelia and I were earnest in our mutual endeavours to benefit our unhappy protégé, and, as a first step to the gradual enfranchisement of his mind, we resolved to divert his attention from those employments, which, like the baneful Oriental drug, destroyed while they excited. For this reason, we strictly forbade his perusal of those tales of toil, of suffering, and of fate, which had hitherto been his chief delight; and while Amelia diverted his attention from those too pleasing themes, she opened to his gaze the inspired tomes of sacred lore, the revealed records of God's chosen people.

All attempts to lead Hayman by the beaten track to an acquaintance with the truths of our religion had hitherto failed, but I now watched with delight his not unwilling progress. His feelings of awe and astonishment at the development of the wonders of the Creation, when the mighty word was spoken, and glad Nature lived; his sympathy, "when the world was all before them"; his grief, when that world was stained with the first brother's blood,

> "And man the sacrifice of man,
> Mingled his taint with every breath,
> Upwafted from the land of flowers."

His lengthened thrill of anguish at the empire of the waters; his rejoicings with the rescued; his wanderings with the "chosen one"; his yearnings at the heart's sacrifice; his sojournings with "the pious." How his eye would sparkle, and his very soul would listen when he, that "loved one," was torn from his father, and from his home, to be Egypt's lord, and to save his father and his kin. And Egypt's magic land, what store of wonders opened fresh to view! The mighty Nile, and mighty Pharaoh, and the humble Moses; God's people—God's power—God's triumph. And he travelled with us forth to the wilderness, and he saw His might, and he reverenced. He heard how the Law was given, amid fire and amid flame, and he, "the meekest man," was unharmed; and the people murmured, and iniquity was punished, and that generation was not. And a new chief arose; and the walls of Jericho trembled—and the sun stood still—and the Lord's name was glorified. Now the people were oppressed, and there rose a deliverer, and the giant champion perished in his pride. And he, the shepherd king, reigned, and angels listened to his harmony, yet he was not worthy, but the wise son built the "house," and even the wisest was won. Then was Israel a kingdom, and the priests ministered, and the inspired prophesied; yet the people did not hearken, and the destroyer came, and the land was desolate, and the city solitary. "By the waters of Babylon we sat down and wept," and the word went out to destroy them, but the hand-writing was on the wall, and the restorer came, and the remnant returned; yet the ancient men wept when the foundation was laid. But the decree had gone forth, and the flock was scattered till the shepherd cometh to call them to the fold.

Hayman listened with intensity to those details, and if he could not sufficiently comprehend their mysteries, yet bowed with submission, acquiescing in the sacred truth of their tenets. For myself, though hitherto I had not swerved in the minutest degree from the strict observance of all the ceremonials of our faith, I must confess, that it was principally this developement of the features of the Jewish religion, that led my mind through its paths of universal love, "from Nature up to Nature's God."

———o———

AN EPITAPH.

"Praises on tombs are idly spent,
A good name is a monument."

One word inscribed will tell Her worth,
Well won in death, as erst at birth;
Immortal honour, deathless fame,
Is Hers, whose life best speaks Her name,

יהודית

Life! with every good entwined,
Kindly heart—expansive mind,
Soul! from earthly passions free,
Vowed, O God! alone to Thee:
E'en as the sun his daily race,
Through heaven's paths his course doth trace;
Wakening into life and light,
Each germ of Nature's blessings bright;
So day by day, and hour by hour,
Emulating Heaven's power;
Pure in thought, in hope, in feeling,
An angel's course on earth revealing;
With one accord did all proclaim,
Well justified that Holy Name,

יהודית

O happy thought! an omen sure,
Of every virtue brightly pure:
Inspired, who guessed thy life-long aim,
A reflex of well-chosen name;
Prophetic, saw thy early youth,
Gemm'd with priceless grace and truth;

Every impulse of whose mind,
With holy aspirations twined ;
Dawnings of that future day,
Thy youth's rich promises repay.
Brightest buds where gently blend,
All to virtuous years that tend,
In every phase of life the same ;
Well honoured thus that sacred name,

יהודית

And well, whose rightly tutored thought,
A fellow soul in faith who sought ;
As kindred plants together twine,
With thine did kindred heart combine.
Like thee with changeless good imbued,
Together then one course pursued,
With faith, that erewhile Israel saw,
Ye firm upheld God's reverent Law ;
Where'er was heard a plaintive sound,
Bounties showering all around ;
Two as one, to aid distress,
Two as one, the poor now bless ;
Sharing in all, whose proudest claim,
Was well to earn that favoured name,

יהודית

From distant lands came danger's cry,
Roused that ancient chivalry,
Which erst in Maccabëan days,
Won for valour deathless praise ;
Bids still the Jew "defend the right,"
And nerved his soul to dare the fight.

Then shrank she cowering from his side?
No! Judith-like, her nation's pride,
With him the threatening danger dared,
With him the fame and glory shared;
In every clime—at Salem's shrine,
Still seeking there for grace divine,
So day by day she thus became,
More worthy of that well won name,

יהודית

Each thought of virtuous life essayed,
Each deed of active good pourtrayed;
By such example, mankind shown,
How best a Jewish heart is known.
The spirit seeks from earth to rise,
Its home in those bright cloudless skies;
Shall we then mourn when Heaven's bloom,
Sheds radiance o'er the dear one's tomb?
Needs there a strain of flattering verse,
Her life-long virtues to rehearse?
One word inscribed will tell her worth,
Well won in death, as erst at birth ;
Immortal honour, deathless fame,
Is hers, whose life best speaks her name,

יהודית

———o———

RHYMES TO THE EYE,

AN ORTHOGRAPHICAL PUZZLE.

I WROTE some lines on a vacant leaf,
To pass the time because I'm deaf;
I showed them to my little daughter,
And saw they filled her full of laughter;
Before she read them half way through,
She said she had of them enough:
She did not wish my pride to wound,
But in them lots of fun she found,
Of mirth there was an ample feast,
Exciting laughter in her breast;
With angry voice and gesture rough,
Seizing the lines I read them through,
When she began to sob and cough;
The tear-drops in her eyelids rose,
For fear my favour she should lose;
She did not wish Papa to plague,
She trembled like one in an ague,
Of tears she shed a streaming flood,
And mournfully before me stood.

Fondly I strove her grief to ease,
And soon to sorrow gave release;
With smiles again my eyes she met,
I gave to her a choice bouquet;
And her spirits to recruit,
A glass of wine and some biscuit;
Showed her models of machines,
Where wondrous skill with art combines,
Sometimes to guide a new-made plough,
Sometimes to mix the baker's dough,

How without the hands to knead,
And cleanly make our daily bread.
Elias Howe's inventions new,
To aid who quickly wish to sew;
A new planned curvilinear arch;
A print of France's stern monarch;
A cheaper plan a hut to thatch;
(I gave her an enamelled watch,
A new-made India-rubber comb,
Engravings of Napoleon's tomb;
And promised, when I'd saved the money,
To buy for her a little poney;)
Told of Pharaoh and his host,
In the depths of Red Sea lost,
Wherein they sank like lumps of lead,
As we in Exodus can read.
I spoke about Sir Walter Scott,
Of Chatham, government depôt,
Of Crœsus, Lydia's monarch rich,
Of Deptford and the famed Greenwich;
About the gentle sainted Agnes,
The price of Clarets and Champagnes.

I showed her Haydn's Book of dates,
And busts of Plato and Socrates,
Statues of a valiant Roman,
Of Joan, that brave devoted woman;
And standing in a hollow niche,
A group of Cupid and his Psyche.
We also spoke of Snowdon's height,
Then of gold's specific weight;
Of the Bank's new rate of discount;
Of Nelson, that chivalric Viscount,

M

Whose valour did in youth appear,
When struggling with a polar bear ;
To board and fight how quick he'd row,
No danger could his courage bow,
Till sad the bullet laid him low :
Where are our naval heroes now ?

Just then came in my daughter's tutor,
He was my dear wife's executor ;
In politics he was a Tory,
His teeth were whiter than ivory ;
A finely chiselled nose and mouth,
He'd scarcely passed the bloom of youth ;
His eyes and hair were darkly brown,
A cloak was o'er his shoulders thrown.
Skilled was he in classic pages,
Knew a dozen languages ;
Well he all his lessons taught,
(I just had paid his quarter's draught ;)
He spoke about the heavenly spheres,
Of Juno, Venus, Mars, and Ceres ;
Like me he never would consent,
Words should have a wrong accent ;
That man, be sure he would indict,
He could of faulty speech convict ;
Most versatile he was in mind,
(A relative of Jenny Lind ;)
Wrote books about the siege of Acre,
Of Saint Bartholomew's massacre,
How the Grecians met their foes,
Then of Helen's brazen shoes,
History's   most   noted   eras,
A *brochure* called "The Two Operas,"

How to cook, preserve, or pickle,
A treatise on the Greek article.
Curious   notions   about   manslaughter,
Which oft provoked my young man's laughter.
I never knew a man alive,
So thoroughly argumentative;
He'd question axioms of Sir Isaac's,
John Stuart Mill's metaphysics;
Denied that Linnæus skill had any,
In   the   principles   of   Botany;
Said the painter's " bits of nature,"
Were like a tawdry caricature;
That Tennyson's verse was weak and flighty,
Ruskin,   in   art,   no   authority;
He stampt each lawyer as a rogue,
Pooh-pooh'd th' Academy's catalogue;
One work he'd praise and never vary,
'T was Doctor Johnson's dictionary.

In the Mediterranean sea,
Near Peninsula of Morea,
As from the deck a storm he watcht,
He fell from off the Fairy yacht;
As his swimming was not strong,
He met his fate the waves among.

When these lines you have read through,
(I wrote them near a Scottish lough,
My cousin sits for the Borough,)
If through them you had time to plough,
Perhaps you've had of them enough;
I'll write some more if you wish, though
I'm troubled with a painful cough,
And sometimes for an hour hiccough.

LOST AND FOUND.

(A HIT OR A BLOT?)

On a steamer, past Gravesend, (how the Hill it is built
    on!)
I was playing Backgammon, (we had just sighted
    Milton,)
My board, overboard, was by heavy draughts tost,
And four or five black men, and Pair-o'-dice Lost.

For our tables to *cater*, came the steward with *trays*;
Some would him *traduce*, but from " gammon " re-
    frained ;
"Give a rope—quick throw—*two sink*—now doubl'
    it," he says ;
On the board placed the black men and Pair-o'-dice
    Regained.

——o——

A PACK OF GOOD FOR NOTHINGS.

(A CYNIC SNARL.)

" He has not a good word to throw to a dog."
                       OLD ADAGE.

Lizzy, you lazy one, out of your bed ;
Sukey, you sulky one, lift up your head ;
Nancy, you noisy one, shut up your jaws ;
Dinah, you dirty one, look at your paws ;

Annie, you artful one, I know your tricks;
You want, long-eared Lyddy, a dozen of kicks;
Jenny, you jealous one, show not such spite;
Look not, proud Mirabelle, black as the night;
Fanny, too frolicsome, stop now your riot;
Maggie and Mattie, you'd better be quiet.
Tilly's too quick, and Milly's too slow;
You're mischievous, Minnie, wherever you go;
Grace, you disgraced yourself, out on the heath—
Who cares for your growl, or your sharp-pointed teeth;
Sally, you silly one, of puppies so fond,
I wish you and they were drown'd in the pond;
In my garden, you, Flora, have trod down the flowers;
Rosa, the rosebuds destroys and devours;
Chloe, you cruel one, killed my canary,
I think none could tame you, except Mr. Rarey;
Phoebe, and Hebe, and Psyche's no good,
And you, dainty Dolly, you sulk at your food;
Cissy and Prissy how reckless you rush,
How wild is your hair—when had you a brush?

But hark! there's the Fox, from your kennels now run,
Up! Hounds! and at 'em! the Hunt has begun.

———o———

FABLE AND MORAL.

(AN EPIGRAM.)

" De te fabula narratur."—HORACE.

FABLES of you are told, you say,
    For such reports pray do not quarrel;
Their untruth I'll at once display,
    For who could find in you a moral?

THE SUIT DISCARDED.

"If you doubt what I say,
Take a bumper and try."
OLD SONG.

"Is it true what I hear you your daughter refuse
 To give to that young man in marriage;
He is rich, he is good, he has excellent views,
 And would buy her her horses and carriage?"

"I admit all you say, and much I regret
 I must still in refusal persist;
He is good, he is learned, he's respectable, yet
 He knows not an atom of whist."

"Not know whist—what a great crime! why should
 that decide?
One moment the marriage delay?"
"Not knowing whist is no crime," the father replied;
 "But at whist he persisteth to play."

—o—

JEW'S MEAT.

(A FACT.)

In a certain country town,
The name of which I need not mention,
There lived "a citizen of renown,"
Whose house required a large extension;
So, blessed with fortune's ample store,
With health and wealth—no child or wife,

He left at once the city's roar,
To taste the sweets of country life.
In this he found a new-born charm,
Kept cows and poultry scarce and big,
And in his well-stocked ample farm
Was nurtured many a well-fed pig.

His kindness he to all extends,
But ere my story I pursue,
Though with his Christian neighbours friends,
Must tell you, Shadrach was a Jew.
That is, he was a Jew by name,
Of Moses' laws performed a part,
Did not his Hebrew birth disclaim,
Like many more, "a Jew in heart."
Respected by his neighbours all,
Mutual presents sent and taken,
He gave them peaches from his wall,
They gave him ham and well-cured bacon.

One time, 'twas in the village known,
(Sent some sharpen'd knives to borrow),
His purpose did his servant own,
To kill two fatted pigs to-morrow;
Unnumbered letters then there came,
Hoping he'd not disappoint,
(Some with baskets filled with game)
Begging he would spare a joint,
From matron, widow, wife, and maid,
And also from the Rector's brother,
"For Jews' meat," they had heard it said,
"Was better far than any other."

MR. NEVILLE.

A TALE IN TWO CHAPTERS.

(FROM AN UNPUBLISHED WORK OF THE AUTHOR'S.)

CHAPTER I.

"The history of that hour unblest,
When like a bird from its high nest,
Won down by fascinating eyes,
For woman's smile he lost the skies."
MOORE.

MR. NEVILLE was a man, whom to see was to admire; there seemed a flow, almost an exuberance of spirits, which diffused a pleasurable sensation wherever he came; it was like the bright and cheerful glow of the well-piled hearth, warming and enlivening. With a fine, bold, though somewhat wrinkled forehead, and an eye whose fire was still undimmed by those years which had shorn his once flowing locks, he would sit the soul and charm of his crowding auditors. Versed in details to please the man or glad the youth, to him the elder came for counsel, the young for advice. Many a thankful heart profited by his suggestions, many a bashful maiden shamed not to make him her confidant. With a glittering toy for the smiling infant, with a marvellous tale for the adventurous boy, the prudence of experience for youth, a kind word for many, a kind deed for all, was it a wonder that he was admired, respected, beloved.

And such a fund of good nature too—not with the sour asceticism which too often in age usurps the place of consistent gravity, he would laugh at the jest, promote the mirth-creating game, or join in the chorus, while he would joke at his own quivering cadences, and tapping his next fair neighbour on the cheek, tell her she should have heard him sing "Fair Chloe" half a century ago. Consequently he was a favourite come where he would, from his jocular disposition, which seemed the very antidote to sadness. Among those by whom he was most esteemed was a Jewish gentleman, who, though firm in his principles, had unhappily formed an attachment to a lady of an opposite faith, and who, at the time of this narrative, was in doubtful deliberation whether to forego his purposed union, or to proceed in what he rightly considered must engender unhappiness to many.

With reluctance did he confide to his venerable friend the workings of his mind. A dull, almost an unearthly paleness came over the countenance of the old man, and the smile which but now had played round his cheek at once saddened into melancholic stupor; but almost immediately rallying, he complained of the cold night air, and proposed a bowl of "policinello," as he jocosely termed it, promising to give his advice on the morrow.

Little inclined for society, yet cheered by the promise of sagacious counsel, and a few friends having arrived, the evening was passed in almost joyous hilarity. Never, as I afterwards learned, did Mr. Neville appear to greater advantage;—he seemed regenerated—a preternatural spring in the wintry season, with mirth-provoking witticisms, lively and shrewd remarks, which each moment elicited; quick, and in varied succession, came lively tale and sportive repartee—jokes and puns in a volley of continued rapidity, and when, in a moment's interval, a half suppressed sigh was heard, on which he was jocosely rallied, it was a prelude to a fresh peal of witticism and laugh-provoking drolleries. He seemed, in fact, the ideality of happiness.

On the morrow, his Hebrew friend, who regretted having asked counsel on a subject, which, though opium-like destroying, he had now resolved not to relinquish, had given orders not to admit any visitors, especially Mr. Neville, whom he was afraid and ashamed to encounter. He was, therefore, surprised and annoyed to be aroused by the friendly salutation of his unwished-for adviser—and rather rudely resented what he now considered an intrusion.

" Nay, nay, my young friend," said Neville, you must not treat me coldly ; I am come to counsel, possessed as I am of your secret. I am come by the right of friendship, by that of sympathy. Nay, you must hear me ; I have no string of reproofs that might offend—I convey no censure—God knows I have no right—no arguments—no tedious reasoning ; I will not tire your ear with my talk. One little tale—you will not refuse to hear it. At least it may amuse a weary hour. You were wont to be somewhat pleased with my recitals. Shall I proceed ?

" In the pleasantest part of the most pleasant county of England, the locality of which is not material to my story, in the twilight of a summer evening, a young traveller was riding homeward, when the hum of music and of mirth caused him to glance at the spot whence those joyous sounds proceeded. On a broad and well-shaded garden terrace, that abutted at a short distance from the main road, was a group that might well excuse a passing gaze of admiration. One beauteous girl stood with arms twined round the marble urn of a sculptured Naiad, into which ever and anon she would dip a sportive hand, and laughingly sprinkle the by-standers. Now peeping from the lime-tree covert, now hiding in the acacia shade, you could see darting forth forms of grace, of mirth, and loveliness, filling the scene with gaiety and joy as they strove to escape the playfulness of their companion. At a little distance, seated under a spreading sycamore, was a gentleman of noble and commanding aspect, gazing with complacency around; near him stood a small knot of musical amateurs, making the air re-echo with the concert of their sweet sounds.

" As the tramp of the steed was heard approaching, a little excusable curiosity prompted some of the fair musicians to lean over the battlemented parapet, and, in their laughing bustle, a guitar fell into the main road. On the stranger perceiving this he alighted, and afterwards standing on the back of his well-trained courser, was enabled to return the instrument to its owner. A smile of thankful acknowledgment was the prelude to a few words of interchanged courtesy, and a brief conversation was terminated by a polite invitation to join the cheerful assembly. Well pleased to be admitted to this lively society, the traveller rode round to the entrance which had been indicated to him, where his steed was tended by a ready domestic, and himself welcomed by the owner of the mansion.

" Often again after this adventure, would our young traveller ride towards the lime-tree fragrance, and often again would a blushing form hang over the marble parapet, welcoming his approach. Acquaintance—inti-

macy—esteem—affection had followed in quick succession; she, the Nymph of the fountain smiled propitious.
He was young, wealthy, the world praised his person
and attainments, and so lively withal, Euphrosyne
might have claimed a foster brother—he seemed, and
he was truly happy.

"Oh! fatal passion, our blessing or our bane—loved
he was; it needs not the dull progressing of rules pre-
scribed to fit us for this mysterious lore; we feel its
electric force, though we cannot reason on its philosophy.
Loved he was; there is a species of freemasonry which
can only be revealed to the initiated—a slight, an
almost imperceptible sign, and we own congenial
sympathy.

"A little month, and he had revealed his secret—he
was a Jew! Nurtured with almost an instinctive
abhorrence for the name, it required all the prepos-
session which had begun to be engrafted in her nature
to repress her feelings on this announcement.

"Her first prejudices overcome gradually, and won by
his earnest beseechings, she yielded an acquiescence to
a purposed plan, which, sanctioned by her friends' consent, would ensure their happiness. I have said our
youth was a Hebrew; one, too, in whom was embedded
a strict devotion to his faith; their union seemed therefore improbable. But a very little reasoning, and her
father and her friends, themselves careless of any faith,
acceded; and a few half muttered, little understood
words, and some trifling formulas sometimes sanctioned
by custom, and she, the fancied convert to Judaism,
became his bride.

"How smoothly blissful then flowed life's current; the days were crested with joy, and time, like

a priceless opal, shone with beauties in every varied aspect.

"To his home he bore her, his fond mother welcomed her new-found daughter, and, well pleased, replied to the thousand questions that were elicited at the novel ceremonies and customs which hourly excited attention. It was little exertion for the young wife to acquiesce in these distinctive rites; pleased at first with their novelty, she now sought the gratification of her fondly attached husband in performing all the minutiæ of her newly adopted faith to the letter.

"To one unacquainted with their origin and intent, there must seem a strange peculiarity in the varied ceremonial observances that are incorporated with the Jewish ritual. Though frequently exciting comment, often ridicule, our young friend had still continued in the practice of every principle and custom, the time-consecrated heirlooms of his creed, and without reasoning too deeply on their mysteries, felt innately convinced that in acting on them he was fulfilling a sacred duty.

"How rejoiced then must he have been to behold his beloved partner seemingly participating in his strict observance, and fondly he imagined faith had engrafted that compliance, which, in fact, was merely effected by her wish to gratify. Nor could it indeed have been expected, that one whose whole life was at variance with her present professions, could at once have entered, with genuine impression, into those so strange, so apparently inconsistent customs. Yet, well-pleased with her willing compliance, it added but another leaf to his wreath of happiness.

*   *   *

"An infant smiling on her mother's breast, another climbing round her lovely neck, two laughing boys playing with her half-loosened tresses, and one, the eldest, a fine lad in embryo military pride, strutting in braided and in plumed attire; the pleased parents' glance oft interchanged, and the yet lover-like tones each other answering—Why should their Paradise have withered?

"Oh! what lovely girls were those sisters of hers, yet how they came, beauteous like the silken store of orient wealth, too oft with pestilence impregnated. From the very hour of their visit and return her whole manner seemed gradually and daily changing. Hitherto she had felt an almost instinctive pleasure in personally superintending many peculiar domestic ceremonials, which the rigid tenets of her husband considered of essential moment; now, relaxing imperceptively, it seemed almost an effort to comply with his wishes in that respect. The aged mother, anxious to hide this neglect from the knowledge of her son, had, by continued exertion, exhausted herself, and her feeble powers wasting, soon ushered her to the tomb.

"Now that none remained to conceal her supineness, daily and hourly did he experience the effects of her indifference to those observances he had hoped she continued to consider as sacred. It is needless to repeat how very important the Israelites conceive to be the retention of those olden usages; they are, in fact, the tenure of their peculiar possession, the feudal homage, time out of mind, offered in grateful vassalage to a mighty Lord, munificent in His privileges, very mild in His expected tribute.

"So years rolled on, instead of the pleased complacency wont to gild each springing hour, came a degree of bickerings and complainings; instead of the candid and the ready reply came equivocating answers or half-murmured denials. From first neglecting his repeated remonstrances, she soon began to ridicule many of his religious forms and practices, and all her inborn feelings rising to her mind, she mocked at those tenets, to him most hallowed. Yet, with all this, he loved her so deeply, that to upbraid seemed as if self-lacerating; and the exertion of authority, which only force could support, was hateful to his thoughts. And when all the brethren of his faith, compelled by her now openly sneering at their peculiarities, shrank from his society, one by one, as they parted, and he looked in her face to chide, some well-remembered grace, some fresh-budding smile, and all his anger was at a glance forgotten. It seemed vain contending with her, such fine-spun webs were woven round him, 'twas powerless as Arachne's skill against the art of Pallas. Wearied with the contest he gradually succumbed.

" What power—how won—how used, it boots not telling—she tempting—he yielding. Day by day relaxing in some minor point, an inroad was advancing in the hitherto impregnable territory. Yet how, as in a faded tapestry, where some less time-worn figure starts in the dim obscurity to light, bringing recollections of what was, so would he, in his downward flight, oft retrace his former views of faith, now in the dim haze quickly vanishing. Bubbles rising on the water's face, floating gossamers on the ambient air, rush more swiftly, rise more thickly, as the air is more disturbed, as the water is more agitated; so is man's mind; placid and content it glides well-pleased with approved theories ; distract it, or with vice or unhappiness, or with folly or crime, and it becomes an arena, wherein the wild and

the strange passions contend for mastery. Acknow-
ledged truths become the sport, oft the victims, of
speculative theory; and the mind which, in prosperity,
was well content to 'stand in awe and sin not,' cannot
cannot now ' be still.' So was it with the somewhile
happy being we speak of; perfect in faith, he doubted
not; why should he doubt, his certainty was happiness;
he has vacillated, and he seeks by fallacious syllogisms
to justify self to self.

"Like those ancient people who used to hide their
gems and gold, lest their morals should be by them
corrupted, so did he feel the stern necessity of banish-
ing himself from her treasured charms, lest their
tempting lures should work to his overthrow. Very
suddenly, and with desperate resolution, did he quit his
native land and depart for an obscure dwelling on the
Continent. Years passed—he heard she was in suffering, wailing his absence, and the doating husband was
again in her arms. His children, they had flown to
welcome him, but when he had blessed them in the
language of the Patriarchs, they had laughed, save one,
and it was he that the mother hated. Their very
father-name too—once borne by sages and heroes, inspiration and valour, had been euphonised; and to all the
remonstrances of their parent were they heedless. How
wretched then was he—all those hopes, that callow
brood he had so fondly nestled, now plumed on their
parting wing! In deference to some remaining embers
of that affection, late so brightly glowing, but which
now, alas! lived only in the half-extinguished ashes, his
once-anxious partner, though she inwardly sneered at
his faith, to the world in some measure concealed how
truly she despised her adopted creed; and now, distant

from her sisters and family, who had removed to the metropolis, she felt it a degree of policy to affect a seeming acquiescence with the practices of those with whom of necessity she was compelled to associate. But all his children, all save one, trained in their mother's secret prejudices, scrupled not, openly by word and conduct to assert their difference of opinions. Gradually withdrawing themselves from the community, they formed ties and connections, which, though no bigot, the father could not behold without heartfelt grief. I have said one son yet remained true to his instilled principles; this, his favoured child, was in consequence so unkindly treated by his brethren and sisters, that he left his home in anger and disgust. Why should I protract? The daughters, how in his heart's core he loved them! scorning a union with worthiness in their father's tribe, became aliens from his home and faith. One son, already half-willingly inclined, was an easy convert to miscalculating zeal, and another, fired with military ardour, had been presented by some friends of his apostate brother with the colours of a marching regiment, and so was the hapless father now bereaved of his children. Desolate indeed was his hearth. In a country town such as the one he inhabited, and where communities watch with a jealous scan, the deviation of his family made him regarded with a supercilious eye by others of his own creed, and his proud nature scorning to justify himself, he seemed almost an outcast to his brethren.

" Sabbaths and holidays wore no longer festal days to him; he could not joy in them alone. He became moody, silent, and abstracted. Then the works of Voltaire and Rousseau were exciting considerable attention;

he glanced at them, at first from curiosity, till attracted
by the theories, to him so novel, he became involved in
a deep consideration of their sophistical doctrines, and
was at every leisure engaged with the dangerous study
of the French and German hollow metaphysics. He
thought their poisons harmless, having as he imagined
an antidote in the strength of his religious principles;
but he knew not that day by day his boasted talisman
was waxing weaker. Against tortures, martyrdom, he
would have triumphed unconquered, but that train of
petty annoyances to which he was now hourly subjected,
wearied and enfeebled him.

" His wedded partner, now almost his sole companion,
whom could he blame for neglect of those minutiæ which,
perhaps, spite of her better feelings, she could not
avoid considering ridiculous? Whom but self? Reared
in a belief so opposite and uncongenial to his own, ought
it to have been a matter of surprise that she should
neglect it? There is a train of intuitive instinct almost
inherent in our nature, which dictates a partiality for
that religion in which we have been born, and under
whose precepts we have been nurtured; and well it
should be so; it is a bond of sympathy attaching friend
and kin; and taught as we are that the pure in all
faiths are equally worthy, the motives that would sanc-
tion a dereliction are such as few can approve. Blinded
in the heyday of youth by the glittering horizon, they
of whom this tale is told, had little thought of the
inevitable change time would bring, or that as sure as
the current which had flowed would ebb, so would, and
so did, the reflux of the tide rush back, surcharged with
the wrecks of its own violence.

CHAPTER II.

"As a beam o'er the face of the waters may glow,
While the tide runs in darkness and coldness below,
So the cheek may be tinged with a warm sunny smile,
Though the cold heart to ruin runs darkly the while."—MOORE.

"WELL! as I have said, immersed in those soul-harrowing applications, his mind's miasma, did he now employ his hours; they had insinuated their venom by slow degrees, but yet not the less noxiously. His faith, the bright armour of his mind, became, as it were, rusted and corroded; those imperceptible fastenings which had held together his protecting mail, became one by one loosened and disunited; and now almost unprotected, he was little able to repel the attacks to which he was consequently subjected. In a word he fell! 'how grand the height from which he fell!'

"It was about this period he began to analyse mysteries his weak mind could not comprehend; and those truths, which the pure light of religion would have shown in their stainless purity, now viewed through the lurid gloom of his tainted atmosphere, were to him shorn of their beaming brightness. Aided by his sophistical studies, he now began to doubt, and cheated by the glitter of their language, he joined with the authors in depreciating and lessening the importance he had hitherto attached to the observances of his forefathers. Now came fallacious reasonings and fine-spun doubting—scepticism with rapid strides advancing, laid its chilling iron hand on his heart, freezing into ice those warm currents of faith and love. In shame, oh, in bitter shame, were the fitful glances he would sometimes take at the past, and he looked back to that

happy time, when, young and haply pure, he walked in
proud belief—but now! And then he would try,
earnestly would he essay, to rise from the thraldom
which overpowered him;

> ' He prayed, he wept, but all in vain;
> For him the spell had power no more;
> There seemed around him some dark chain,
> Which still as he essayed to rise,
> Baffled, alas! each wild endeavour.'

" She died—a severe and prolonged illness, contracted
at some new-sprung sectarian meeting to which she had
attached herself, consigned her to eternity. He gazed
on the pallid form lying before him, and ' like a tomb-
searcher memory ran,' and he thought on the joyous
hours of their early years—their happiness—their
misery; how happy had each been asunder—how
wretched together. Could he then, with the dead
before him but grieve, from all estranged. Oh, he did
grieve, bitterly—bitterly, that wretched man—hot
scalding tears, that quench not but scorch—with one
clasped hand linked in with the dead.—Sir, sir, had you
seen him then, as the commingling thoughts of past
and present came rushing—years of agony in one hour
—trembling limbs faltering with fierce emotion—fixed
and blood-shot eyeballs straining with internal anguish
—convulsive pangs of a bursting brain—suffocating
breath-stifling throbs that checked even the attempt
at prayer—quivering creepings of the flesh—tortures of
the palsied heart—be there angels would they not
have pitied? demons, would they not have compas-
sionated? She was buried at her own dying request in
the churchyard of her native village. The bereaved
husband had promised in her last moments, to accompany her to the tomb. Sufficient of his ancient feelings

remained to induce a degree of repugnance at inter-
mingling in the religious rites of another creed, yet it
was astonishing with what a degree of indifference he
entered an edifice he would, till now, have considered it
idolatry to have gone to.

To him now seemed alike, and alike unimportant, or
synagogue, or church, or mosque, or conventicle; the
serpent-winding had encircled him, had poisoned, had
crushed. It was here for the first hour, for many years,
he met his children, her children; here over her grave
they hung around him as in youth's time, striking the
hardened rock of paternal emotion, that now gushed
forth streams of affection and forgiveness. From the
grave he almost mechanically accompanied his daughters to their homes, and won by their entreaties, was
prevailed on to remain a permanent guest with the
youngest in the metropolis. I need not tell you, that
every custom, rite, and distinction was now forgotten;
reckless, indifferent to him, were alike unheeded, or
holy days, or holy deeds, remembered records of olden
time, venerable monuments, time's landmarks, proofs of
faith, most ancient, most divine.

"Now, shaming, he felt ashamed at all that should
call the past to mind; carefully avoiding intercourse
with all who might recall uncongenial thoughts, he
mixed little with society; the proud heraldry of his birth
was despised and cast away, and he sought by a flimsy
disguise to hide from the world his parentage and
descent.

So manhood withered; led by false meteors, pestilen-
tial vapours, that shone as in mockery of heaven's
beams—shall I disguise it?—in effect he became a
sceptical unbeliever, an all-doubting theorist; and his
few friends, and his very children, shrunk in horror

from the impious ravings of distorted reasoning; and
after a brief contention, he, the misanthrope, was again
alone.   Prostrating sickness came, with sickness came
repentance ; not that real remorse, the offspring of conviction, but that bastard sorrow, engendered of weak-
ness and of fear.   Untended couch, save by menial's
hand ; wasting strength, uncheered by kindly word ;
the mind's disease, unministered to, corrupting ; and
that soul-healing panacea, religion's balm, as if in
mockery, starting to his lips, to be by some hidden
power withdrawn.

"He recovered ; ' *Carpe diem* ' was now his maxim ;
what had he to do with the future, the future that
chance might never come ; cunningly he masked his
agitations ; he disguised the habitants of his soul,
those Gorgons that had petrified his heart to stone, and
with rare cosmetic skill, filling their wrinkles, the
world took them for Graces.   Everywhere he came now
people envied his joyousness, and noted him happy ;
they saw the flowers, not the grave they o'ershadowed ;
they saw the glittering gems, not the scars they hid ;
the rippling waves, not the wreck they covered ; alone,
alone, it was he thought, and the reaction of his
assumed joy was thereby the more wretched.   ' It is
an opinion,' says Locke, ' that the soul always thinks.'
Truly did he feel this assertion.

*   *   *

"At the door of a physician's reception room, a
patient, the physician's friend, recognised an old man,
one, whose tale of depression and mental wretchedness
had excited the compassion, even of the well-schooled
practitioner.   To shame his friend's fancied maladies,
the physician had related to him those truly agonising
symptoms he just with pain had heard.   And to wile

him from his hypochondriac dulness, asked his company to the festal board of a mutual acquaintance, where, said he, 'I am invited to meet, for the first time, one, whose mirth and cheerfulness would be of more service in dispelling sadness, than all the drugs in the Pharmacopœia.'

" ' And that happy man, that care-dispeller, by what name shall I hail him ? '

" ' His name is Neville.'

" ' Good God! 'tis his misery you just have told me; 'twas Neville I met at your threshold.' "

Here the old man paused abruptly from excitement and exhaustion, and fell death pale on the sofa, with clasped hands, ashy lips, and a face of marble coldness. By the constant application of ether and other restoratives, he was recalled to consciousness.

" Yes! it was Neville, it was I; it was mine the tale you have heard, it was mine the misery you have known; I have cut deep, that you might trace the source of the gangrene; I have bared the veins that you might see them festering. My race on earth is run, the curtain is dropped, and the actor's part is over. When that you saw me joyous, knew you my agony? when that you heard my laughter could you have known its hollowness? Oh! she was fair and beautiful as the young sun of the morning—then she was cold, and I followed her to the grave; on earth is none to me, what have I to hope, doubting heaven? Young man, I have done a fearful and a burning penance in this my history. I have offered it in expiation—may it be accepted. I smile no more. It were less pain to me weeping than seeming gladness. I see you trembling on the unknown precipice, I offer you the hand to save you from the gulf. Will you refuse the aid? You

are young and happy now—so was I; blessed in faith—
so was I; I lost my faith, I lost my happiness; and
when myself sinking, did I not drag another down to
destruction? To-morrow's sun, and I leave England
for ever, with not even a parting word from any—and
I have children. I have seen them as times they have
passed me unheeding, and I have that day been more
loud in voice, and more mirthful in tone, but it was as
the vulture screech o'er the rankling carcase. "Farewell! you have heard my tale—yourself apply the moral."

So saying the old man rose, and refusing assistance,
left the house. He was never seen again.

———o———

A PETRIFACTION.

"No aid can I give your Asylum to build,"
    Said Gripus, from cash loth to part,
"To pray your good wishes may all be fulfilled,
    I assure you, you have all my heart."
"With thanks o'en this gift we grateful receive,
    Our expenses so largely have grown;
Your heart it is welcome, for now we perceive
    'T will save us a trifle in stone."

———o———

A PRECEDENT.

To rise to an office you long time have sought,
    And pompous pretensions you force;
You'll succeed—for it's just to my memory brought
    That Caligula ennobled his Horse.

THE MERRIMENT OF . SADNESS.

"Mirth to madness near allied."

Come let's be merry once again ;
The lively song and the sportive strain
　　Shall usher in the dance ;
And the flowing bowl, and the sparkling cup,
Shall rouse my sleeping spirit up,
　　And wake me from my trance.
And we'll be merry—O ! so glad ;
'Twould drive e'en joyous Momus sad
　　To see himself outdone ;
Such mirth and jollity and glee,
Though Dian shall our revels see,
　　We'll hail the rising sun.

And our wine—O ! our wine shall be
　　The very best ;
And the creaming bowl, still full and free,
　　Shall give its zest.
And so merrily we'll laugh and drink,
Who'll dare, who'll dare, to-night to think,
　　Of future or of past ?
What though the thorn is in my soul,
The rose is swimming in my bowl,
　　I'll drink while yet it last.

And we'll toast—oh ! we'll toast to-night,
　　The brightest eyes ;
And smiles and lips that call to light,
Imagination's fancies bright,
　　Of Paradise ;

And we'll hang, we'll hang, a glittering veil,
  O'er by-gone years,
And our barks shall float in a spicy gale,
With gilded prow and silken sail—
  We'll have no tears.

We'll have no tears—O! no, not we;
Why should our glad revels be
Check'd with plaint of misery,
  Or doleful voice of woe?
We laugh at all those trifles now,
The broken heart—forgotten vow—
The wasted cheek, the sadden'd brow;
  We'll have no tears, O no.

Plighted vows—say what are they?
A girlish sport, a maiden's play;
Lightest words and lightest spoken,
Sportive given—sportive broken:
Flowers—when with their fragrance cloyed,
How easily are they destroyed;
And even if a leaf should linger,
The softest breath, the lightest finger,
Can brush the intruder far away,
To trample it beneath the clay.

And broken hearts—I laugh to think
How easily each link by link
Of chains that seemed so close entwisted,
As if but one the two existed,
Can be by gentlest hands untied,
Or words more sharp than swords divide.

And then that man should be so vain,
To think pledged troth a binding chain,
Or that he e'er a tie could find,
Would fix the faith of womankind.

The chain is off my soul, but still
The canker rust its furrows fill;
And o'er its course my life-tide's flood
Mingles the iron with my blood.
Fill! fill! to the broken heart;
Come hither, come hither, my own sweet love;
See on my cup bright Venus' dove,
Nestles to bless us ere we part;
Come kiss me, sweet; aye, this is kind;
Your hands are raised my eyes to blind,
And while repeated kisses speak,
I see not your averted cheek.
O! this is kind—for still you seem,
The spirit of my brightest dream;
Now once again—embrace—we part—
Fill! fill! to the broken heart!

Fill! fill! whose was that sigh?
Again—'tis false—it was not I;
Where's the silly fool who sighs
While from his cup the sparkle flies.
I sighed not—it was I who laughed,
As long and deep the bowl I quaffed;
Strange to me you can't descry,
The difference of a laugh or sigh.
I laughed, I laugh—what will you more—
Still each time louder than before;

Though chance from me each merry sound,
Upspringing from an Upas ground,
My heart's taint mingling with my breath,
Give mirthful notes the tone of death.

Fill! fill! what have we here?
Nay, nay, indeed 'tis hardly fair;
What frolic could you now design
To change my ruby-sparkling wine,
To bitter gall and salty brine,
And tell me that the cup is mine?
What though one tear my cheek did burn,
That single drop could never turn
My sparkling cup erewhile so clear.
Well—heed it not—though brine and gall,
Give me the cup, I'll drain it all;
And freshly as my heart-drops fall
At memory's ever-wakening call,
The bitter draught my soul shall cheer.

Not bitters—but the sweetest sweet,
Mix to make my soul complete;
Balmy words and honied smiles,
Shame the sweets of western Isles;
Nectar draughts still fraught with bliss,
Teeming in each long-drawn kiss;
And fruitful hopes and roseate hours,
Crown my bowl with wreathing flowers;
With memory's dreams hope yet endears,
My sweetest draught, of bitter tears.

Bumpers! I've a toast to-night,
And sure you'll do my bidding right;
Charge! fresh wine—fresh goblets—fill,
He is my foe who lingers still.

All ready ! rise ! and three times three,
Drink ! though the drink should hemlock be ;
My love ! my first, my last !
What now ! what now ! my cup is full,—
Great God ! I'm drinking from a skull.

Come pass the wine, the joke, the song,
Give the chorus loud and long ;
A round, a round of mirth and glee,
My voice shall still the loudest be ;
You never heard at a funeral
A priestly voice more loud and full ;
You never heard the screech-owl cry,
A higher strain than now do I ;
I'm loud ! I'm loud ! then who dare say,
That mine is not a merry lay ?

Give me the wine ! My soul has quaffed
Elysian drink, Lethëan draught.

With kind oblivion, see, there came
Regeneration through my frame ;
And see you not my placid brow,
And smiling cheek—I'm happy now.
O ! so happy !—where's my wreath ?
Inhaling its soft balmy breath,
I care not were an asp beneath ;
   The rose is blushing to my view,
   The flowers in bright and morning dew,
   And every bud still fresh and new :
      I'm happy—happy now.

O! so happy! bright and brief
Shone the buds in that fairy wreath,
But the serpent's slime was on each leaf;
　　The wreath is gone—what need I care;
　　Each thorn that stripped my forehead bare,
　　Can tell how firm the rose *was* there:
　　　I'm happy—happy now.

More wine! more wine! another wreath!
What! all the flowerets gone?
There surely is enough for one,
That mouldering tomb beneath;
Now this is well, and in my bowl,
The hellebore shall swim,
While poppies floating to the brim,
Give slumber to my soul.

Sing! sing! not you, nor you, but she,
Whose every word is minstrelsy;
She! whose notes I long have heard,
While ears drank deep each hallowed word;
And hark! I hear that voice again,
Echoing each remembered strain,
To which so oft I sat and listened,
While pleasure's gems my eye-lids glistened;
I hear once more that gladsome strain,
And scarce my throbbing heart contain;
But yet my love it seems to me,
Each song, erewhile so full of glee,
All saddened o'er with anguish now,
Belies thy smiling cheek and brow:
　　　Give o'er—give o'er,
　　　We'll sing no more.

Now am I not a jovial host?
Who says I'm sad? I've drunk the most.
What to you, so my cup o'erflows,
That my heart is chilled with wintry snows?
You are not half so gay as I,
Your wine is gone—your goblet dry;
For shame! for shame! come, fill and drink,
Is this a time for us to think.

Huzza! advance! come join the dance,
    And wile away the night;
See a throng, they trip along,
    Nature's beauties bright.
I see! I see! and I and she,
    With every sense entranced,
We hail again, that joyous strain,
    To which we oft have danced.

Closer, closer, while our hands are pressing,
Brief, but very exquisite that blessing,
"List thee, dearest, echoing pulses beat,
And raptured thoughts our answering looks repeat,
Nor words, nor looks, can tell thee what I feel;
Why need I tell, what I could ne'er conceal;
For love, give love, and fill my hopes of bliss;
That smile, that blush, that look, that thrill, that kiss."

Hark! unto that dreadful crash,
    Is that the thunder's roar?
Fearful I see the lightning flash,
    Reveal the vacant floor.

Pshaw! I've been dreaming, boys,
  Where is the wine?
Here's to your health, my boys,
  Pledge me now mine;
Here's to each dear delight,
  Once we have known;
O! they were fair and bright—
  Where have they flown?

Come, fill again, Aurora's hair
Streaks with light the morning air;
She shall never say that we
Blushed to bear her company;
Like morning's golden tints now see,
Our bright Champagne and Burgundy;
And now her veil aside she throws,
Blushing like a new-born rose,
Her roseate colours paint the sky—
We've ruby wine with her shall vie.

Have we not been joyous—merry?
Indeed, I know that I have—very;
Is there the gloom upon my brow?
What cause have I for sadness now?
My very heart and soul are glad,
'Tis only parting makes me sad.

And now we part, yet once again
The sparkling bowl my lips shall drain,
And spare the words would doleful tell
To mirth and love a sad farewell.

———o———

"EX FUMO DARE LUCEM."

THOUGHTS SUGGESTED BY THREE CHIMNIES AT A BIRMINGHAM
FACTORY.

Musing in my solitude, around I cast my glance,
And listless to the passing world, unheeded Time's
advance;
I gazed, almost unconsciously, at every bustling scene;
I saw, but yet scarce seemed to see, the heaven's bright
serene;
Yet as I gazed, methought there came, unbidden to
my call,
New lessons fraught with wisdom's lore, from yon three
chimnies tall;
E'en mid their smoke, that dimmed the air, and clouded
o'er the sky,
"Sermons in stones," as men can find, so, there might
we descry
Comparisons might wake the sense and animate the
mind,
Might show some phase of new-born light, some image
of mankind.

In that tall column, mounting there, as though 't would
cleave through space,
Upwards, unchecked, its spiral dart, now heavenwards
we trace;
No wind can stem its proud design, no zephyrs tempt
to swerve,
One bold grand volume still upsprings, nor checked by
break or curve.

o

So mounts the mind of man, impelled by ambition's
    daring call;
So triumphs he of bold intent, nor fears he e'er may fall;
So rises he to height of power; so he with angels vies;
And so, he men of meaner mould, doth scornfully
    despise.

—o—

Unsteady, curling, wreathing waves, that swell from
    yonder shaft,
Now yielding to each petty breeze, now swayed by
    every draught,
Ere yet our eye can trace a course, in circling eddies
    caught,
Fantastic motions cheat the sight, then vanish into
    nought;
How like the man of wavering mind, devoid of fixed
    design,
Who yields to every soft impress—or hers—or yours—
    or mine;
No bright ambition fills his soul, but idle pleasures
    wreathe
Their web of golden gossamer, wherein content to
    breathe,
He wastes his noble energies, and like a failing stream,
So passes life in vapoury deeds—so fades away his
    dream.

—o—

Now here, now there, a cloudy smoke, a pillar murky
    black,
With undulating motion moves, like serpent's stealthy
    track,

Awhile some purpose seems to guide its course, now
    eastward bent,
Then sudden changing in its point, on westward mis-
    sion sent,
Its eddies whirl a sooty shower, and darken all with
    gloom ;
No tapering column cheers the view, but restless
    changeful fume.
Here view the man whom fortune guides, if steadily
    he'd woo,
One course of honest industry—that course alone pursue,
Nor when he sees his neighbour thrive, would envious
    turn his will,
To emulate that neighbour's art, in which he boasts
    no skill ;
His own employ he thus neglects—his own enjoyments
    · fail,
Fell darkening ruin's saddened cloud will o'er his path
    prevail,
And where he tracks his restless road, will misery mark
    the trail.

——o——

E'en as I mused, the evening bell to toil now gave
    release,
For lengthening shadows on the wall, foretold the hour
    to cease ;
The doors flung wide, and streaming forth, from fac-
    tories' hot control,
A tide of human waves poured forth in one continuous roll ;
And there were stalwart artizans, with heavy work
    outworn,
And yet the curse of Adam's race they knew must still
    be borne,

And there were hoary locks, snow-flakes, that hovered
    o'er the grave,
Yet sad they toiled, those aged men, their little life to
    save.
And woman's gentle voice was heard, in feeble tones,
    yet mild,
Encouraging with its dulcet words, her overworken
    child.
Their day of labour now is o'er, their hard-earned pit-
    tance won,
Again must be that race of toil, with morrow's dawn
    begun.
No sound of gladness greets the ear, too tired is hand
    and will,
The sunless sky is black and void—the freshened air
    one chill.
And so they totter, dirt-begrimed, with pale and
    saddened looks,
And scarce a word of greeting fond, the wearied hus-
    band brooks ;
All prostrate there is might and skill, their strength is
    now o'erwrought;
And powerful men, all feeble now, like powerless
    infants brought.
"Is this," I cried, "the sole foredoom of man to sweat
    and toil,
To bend beneath this yoke of pain, this endless sad
    turmoil.
The sacred spirit that partook, in man's first primal birth,
Is it for ever doomed to toil, as if it too were earth?"

Yet, as I spoke, a glorious burst of heaven's richest light,
Pierced through the distant horizon, in glittering
    radiance bright;

It seemed a soft remonstrance mild, yet tempered all
 with love,
Whose tones would fain repress the thoughts they could
 not but reprove ;
What various tints of roseate hue, what glorious Tyrian
 dye,
Pervade in all their gorgeousness, the western evening
 sky ;
A molten mass, in fusion rare, new brightnesses arrange,
Still changeful in their varied forms, celestial in each
 change ;
And see! though wearied with his toil, that burly
 workman pause,
And lift his eyes in gratitude, to Thee, Thou Great
 First Cause ;
The old man shows the little child, as though he would
 him teach,
To strive to gain that heaven bright, now almost in his
 reach ;
The mother thankful views the group, and twines her
 welcome arms,
Around her husband's cheerful form, who now slights
 not her charms.
New life, new vigour now inspired, a merry laugh
 breaks out,
And friends meet friends, and kindred, kin, with mirth
 and joyful shout.
And so the evening sun went down in his rich crimson bed,
Yet lingering rays of light and life, around are every-
 where shed.
Then spoke my soul, " Though man on earth to toil
 for bread be driven,
His spirit soars to seek his home, for endless life in
 Heaven."

THE HIDDEN FUTURE.

הנסתרות לה׳ אלהינו

"Heaven from all creatures hides the book of Fate."
POPE.

In vain we ask; no eye can pierce the veil,
  That mercy hangs to shroud our future fate;
No tongue can tell the yet unfashioned tale,
  No lips the yet unacted deeds relate;
Vainly delusive, hope bright fabrics builds,
  Vainly deluding, roseate visions gleam;
Cheating the sense imagination gilds
  A false and fleeting meteoric beam.
All, all in vain, wearied the anxious thought,
  Strives ineffectual through the gloom to trace;
Man's feeble light is vainly glimmering brought
  To wake the mystery of the viewless space.
Gay flowers to pluck they haste, and grasp but weeds;
  Loved words to hear, where mocking echoes speak;
Fond smiles to greet, where scowling hate recedes;
  Bright lips to kiss, an aspic stings the cheek;
For changed or changing, e'en as lightning quick,
  Ere yet conceived, the hours their courses run,
Faint shadowy visions, clust'ring fast and thick,
  Ere bright yet dark, concluded ere begun.

Round the closed portals of impervious fate,
  Crowding, men seek to pierce the darksome gloom;
Oracular they speak with fond hopes elate,
  Frail hopes that wither in the early tomb.
Honours and riches in the distance float,
  Glory and power glide on in fancy's dream;
Distant yet present, near, yet how remote,
  The spectre barks that fill that mirage stream.

How well withheld!   When scintillates with light,
　The blue serene that knows no envious cloud,
Why sad foresee the shades of coming night,
　Or darkening mist the heavenly orbs enshroud?
That dear first child who climbs the father's knee,
　In whose embrace the mother's heart is blest,
Whose future life one endless joy to see,
　Fills with prophetic hope each parent's breast,
Would it be well to antedate the time,
　Those hopes o'ercast, and when with failing breath,
Too early lost he withers e'er his prime,
　Or better than his life were e'en his death.
Would it be well, when hand in hand ye twine,
　Two souls as one, ye start on life's career,
The aspirations of your thoughts combine,
　This earth a foretaste of the heavenly sphere.
Would it be well, that time, alas! to know,
　When she you fondly cherished all your own,
Changes from summer smiles to wintry snow,
　And leaves your martyred heart to die alone.

Our lives form part of one harmonious whole,
　Still dare the race, in all foresee the best,
Strive for the good, speed on to reach the goal,
　And leave to His just will to guide the rest.
God's laws revealing, veiled, e'en Moses stood—
　If God conceals His purpose here below,
Be sure Omniscient thought best understood,
　What well to hide, and what we best should know.
Could wisdom see the toil of midnight hours,
　New fangled schemes of puerile folly mock,
Would wisdom waste his energetic powers,
　The statue ne'er had left the marble rock.

Ye mighty minds that skilful fertilise
    With plenteous seed the erewhile barren soil,
Harvests anticipated greet your gladsome eyes,
    And well repay your patient laboured toil,
If blight or blast, mildew or stunted yields,
    Ye had forethought, perchance benignant now,
The mellow grain would never gild the fields,
    Or fill the furrows of the expectant plough.
"Cowards die many times before their death;"
    Irresolution, ill presaging, lies inert;
Weak doubt enfeebling comes with chilling breath,
    How can the fettered limbs their strength exert?
Bolder his course whose purpose nobly bent,
    Whate'er befalls, strives on in hopeful ease,
Beholds the present filled with good intent,
    And trusts the future to His just decrees.
Mystery impenetrable! well dost Thou conceal,
    What could we see would every hour enshroud,
What strength would weaken grief to bliss reveal,
    And leave the lonesome heart with sorrow bowed.
Our joys were shadows could we antedate,
    Our pains were doubled could we them foresee;
Omniscient! well dost Thou control our fate,
    And best our trust, confiding best in Thee.

FINIS.